To Kris

POPPY'S PROPOSAL

TARA GRACE ERICSON

Be a wildflower:
Stand tall,
Be persistent, and
Seek the light.

Tara Grace Ericson

SILVER FOUNTAIN PRESS

Copyright © 2020
Tara Grace Ericson and Silver Fountain Press
All rights reserved.

No part of this book may be used or reproduced in any manner whatsoever without written permission, except in the case of brief quotations embedded in critical articles and reviews. The unauthorized reproduction or distribution of this copyrighted work is illegal. No part of this book may be scanned, uploaded or distributed via the Internet or any other means, electronic or print, without the author's permission.

This book is a work of fiction. The names, characters, places, and incidents are products of the writer's imagination or have been used fictitiously and are not to be construed as real. Any resemblance to persons, living or dead, actual events, locale or organizations is entirely coincidental. The author does not have any control over and does not assume any responsibility for third-party websites or their content.

Paperback ISBN-13: 978-1-949896-14-5
Ebook ISBN-13: 978-1-949896-11-4

To Jessica, whose excitement about this project sometimes exceeded my own.
This one is for you!

"And we know that for those who love God all things work together for good, fo those who are called according to his purpose."

— Romans 8:28

CONTENTS

PROLOGUE

Laura Bloom sprinkled a handful of flour across the counter and waved her hand across the cool dusty surface to spread it evenly. She picked up the silky dough and stretched it gently against the granite. Grabbing her trusty rolling pin, she added a pinch of flour to it before rolling the dough into a large rectangle.

She had made these same cinnamon rolls hundreds of times over the years, but the reactions from her children made the extra work worthwhile. Homemade cinnamon rolls were a perennial favorite at Bloom family brunch. Over the years, Saturday morning breakfast had become a veritable tradition, and it was rare for one of her children to miss it.

Poppy wandered in, groggily reaching for a mug and pouring a cup of coffee. "Good morning, Poppy."

"Morning, Mom. Need any help?"

Laura shook her head, and Poppy sat at a barstool across the counter. It was still early; in a few hours this kitchen would bustle with activity. Laura knew Poppy sometimes felt overlooked. It was easy to be lost in the shuffle of seven children. Hawthorne always stood out as the only boy. Daisy and Dandelion, her twins, had each other. As the oldest, Lily kept her share of the spotlight. And as the youngest, Rose did too. But Lavender and Poppy? They were quieter, more introspective, but no less treasured by their parents or siblings. Poppy's deep feelings also came with feisty reactions and a sharp-tongued wit.

Taking advantage of a few moments alone with Poppy, Laura asked, "All ready for Apple Days this weekend?"

Poppy nodded, "Yep. Should be all set. Are you still able to help coordinate the vendors?"

Laura nodded. "I'll be there. You've done a wonderful job, Poppy."

"Lily helped with the event stuff. I just grow the apples."

"We all know that isn't true, sweetheart."

Her daughter sighed. "I know, Mom. It just

sometimes feels like I'm not doing enough, you know? Does our little farm here really matter? I love this farm more than anything in the entire world, but I wonder if I should be doing more?"

As Laura sprinkled generous handfuls of cinnamon and sugar over the buttered dough, she glanced up at her daughter, meeting the dark eyes she inherited from her father. "Poppy, if you've been called to cultivate the land, then that is enough. What you've done with Bloom's Farm is amazing. You should be so proud. Your father and I are." Then, Laura asked, "Do you think you've been called to something else?"

Poppy shook her head, "No, nothing like that. Don't worry about me, Mom. It's just early morning blues. I'm going to take a shower before breakfast." With that, her daughter disappeared back to the basement. Laura whispered a quick prayer. Despite her efforts and ownership of the farming operations, Poppy was searching for something, waiting for something. Laura just didn't know what. So she was trusting God.

It was an intense honor to watch her child so lovingly nurture the farm and the plants. What an amazing mother Poppy would be. But so far, there was no man in Poppy's life. And other than the over-the-hill farmhands Poppy managed, there was not much hope of meeting anyone with her feet so deeply rooted in the soil of Bloom's farm. Laura felt a nudge that her daughter would leave the farm. It seemed hard to imagine, but it felt true. What could make Poppy leave her family and the farm she loved so much?

1

Harrison Coulter stared across the conference table at Neil Powers, his political advisor. Neil had approached him seven years ago about running for office. Now, his friend and colleague begged him to reconsider his plea.

"Harrison, this is your only option. Unless you get married before announcing your candidacy for governor, it is a complete non-starter. The party will not support you." Neil ran a hand through his thinning hair.

Harrison shook his head and twisted the pen in his hands. "I just don't understand. Didn't you say I was everything the party was looking for? Unless I'm single." He frowned at Neil's nod. This was ridiculous. Harrison hadn't even wanted to go into politics.

After college, he became a lawyer because he had a love for justice. And partly because he loved to argue.

Neil stood and paced the small conference room. "You *are* everything they are looking for, Harrison. But the voters in our wonderful state simply will not elect a 32-year-old bachelor to the highest office in the state government. They will not do it. So either you wait and miss this election cycle, or you get married. And if you miss this time around, it's eight years before we get another shot."

"Neil, I'm not even dating anyone. How am I supposed to get married?" Did they think he could summon a wife out of thin air?

"I know that. Do you think I don't know that?" Neil looked to Harrison's Chief of Staff. Bethany Williams was old enough to be Harrison's mother, and she had been around the state government of Indiana since before he was born. Somehow, he hit the lottery when she agreed to come work for him. "Back me up on this, Bethany."

The ever-practical woman held up her hands, "Don't rope me into this, Neil."

Harrison smiled at her no-nonsense tone. Let's see how far Neil had thought this out. "Okay, okay. Let's say I agree with you—that I don't think I can get elected unless I'm married. What do you think I should do?" Harrison had been in politics for six years, which was almost nothing in this world of career politicians. But, much to his surprise, he relished the opportunity to create lasting changes for the people of this state. When Neil first approached him, Harrison had just landed a major court victory for exposing fraud and injustice within the city government. Harrison said no, repeatedly. Until his pastor urged him to pray about it. And wouldn't you know it? God affirmed the path.

On especially difficult days, when he was tired of the negotiations and political drama, Harrison asked God the question again, hoping he had completed the mission. So far, he had only been told to stay. Harrison wasn't sure yet if God was telling him to run for governor, but he wasn't sure He wasn't. He would keep asking, but Harrison needed to know what it would take.

"You need a wife. Right? In this political arena, you are still positioned as the home-grown country boy who made a name for himself. Your wife needs to be someone who shares that heritage. Someone who loves Indiana as much as you do. Someone voters will love." Neil raised an eyebrow at him, "Someone people would believe you fell for."

Harrison snorted.

Sure, they could pull a perfect Miss Indiana out of a box and he would propose next week. Still, as Neil continued to describe his ideal candidate, Harrison's mind wandered about 200 miles west of his current Indianapolis office back home to a little speck on the map, fifteen miles from anywhere. There was a girl he knew like the one Neil was describing.

The only problem was, Poppy Bloom was unlikely to vote for him, let alone marry him.

Poppy strolled through the annual pick-your-own apple event, watching it unfold with pride on the outskirts of the orchards in the freshly mowed pasture. Each year, Apple Days grew. This year, Poppy invited local craftsmen and businesses to set up booths and carnival games for families. Plus she was selling the apple butter, pie filling, and cider from this year's harvest.

Her sister Daisy manned the cash register, weighing apples and ringing up jelly jars. Another sister clutched her camera tightly, snapping pictures of the event. Lavender's hard work as their marketing expert was a huge reason events like Apple Days succeeded. Poppy stepped next to her younger sister and laid a hand on her shoulder. "Great turnout, isn't it?"

Lavender nodded, watching a group of children play catch with a bright red apple. "The Facebook event got a lot of reach."

"Well, thanks for everything you do. I think these types of events are exactly what Bloom's Farm needs to do more of. It's so important that kids know where their food comes from." Even here in western Indiana, in the heart of American farmland, too many children would never plant a garden or taste a fresh-picked tomato. It made Poppy want to invite every single one out to the farm.

A shadow fell over her shoulder, and she turned to see the county commissioner, Gerald Ruiz, and greeted him.

"Well, hello, Miss Bloom. Fine event you've got here."

"Thank you, Commissioner. How are things at the county these days?"

"Oh, you know. Mostly the same, although I recently heard of something you might be interested in. You know my family sold our farm a few years back, but I would never want to see anything happen that would threaten small, family-owned farms."

Warning bells sounded in her head. Anything that threatened small farms was something she would fight against tooth and nail. "What are you talking about?"

"Oh, just some new proposals over in Indianapolis. I guess those big farm corporations have deep pockets with more than one senator in them." The Commissioner told Poppy about a new piece of legislation. From the sound of it, The Farm Business Act would strip away financial incentives for smaller farms and give a huge advantage to larger, single-crop operations.

If Poppy's understanding of this train wreck was accurate, it would mean the end of small farming operations like hers and hundreds of others in the region.

Bloom's Farm was known for growing a wide variety of crops with a low environmental impact philosophy. Farmer's markets and Community Supported Agriculture Programs were the lifeblood of her operation. The CSA produce baskets encompassed Poppy's priority to provide local produce and partner with families directly. She had worked hard to convince her father that moving toward organic, diverse produce was the best business move. If The Farm Business Act succeeded, it could mean the end of the Bloom's Farm she had worked so hard to create. Now, she just had to figure out how to stop it.

"I had no idea, Commissioner." Poppy said honestly. There had been a little buzz on the online farming forums, but nothing so drastic.

"I'm sure it will be okay, Miss Bloom. Your farm here is a local landmark. I can't think of a better way to spend a Sunday afternoon." She smiled tightly as the commissioner saw a familiar face and strolled across the pasture with an arm raised in greeting.

Whatever the Commissioner thought, this was not okay. Maybe Bloom's Farm would survive. With Lily's event barn, animals, and the bed-and-breakfast, they were better off than most farms. But her friends? Poppy needed to stop this bill. The state senate wasn't in session until January. That was months away, but the clock had started ticking.

Sunday night, Poppy built a small campfire as Lavender fiddled with a Bluetooth speaker from the truck bed parked nearby. This small creek and makeshift beach had seen thousands of Bloom family campfires over the years. Tonight, it hosted Mandy Elliott's bachelorette party. S'mores, camp chairs, and a 90s boy band playlist was the perfect way to celebrate their friend's upcoming marriage.

Poppy would regret staying up too late and eating far too many processed foods, but as the laughter rang out over the quiet pasture behind them, she couldn't regret the evening. Daisy was the Maid-of-Honor, and their friend Chrissy was a bridesmaid. Chrissy had her own wedding in just a few weeks, too. In fact, the only single ladies at the party were from the Bloom Family—Poppy and her sisters. Maybe it was a family curse.

"Okay, Mandy. Tell us the truth," Daisy called from across the circle. "How did you meet Dr. Pike?"

Mandy covered her face with her hands and the others encouraged her, "Come on, tell us."

"There's a reason I haven't said anything. It's embarrassing!" she admitted.

Another friend from Minden, Charlotte, chimed in, "It can't be more embarrassing than when I assumed Luke was breaking into Ruth's cabin."

Lavender delicately placed a marshmallow on a skewer. "That's nothing. Daisy fell through the ceiling while Lance was in the room below her." Daisy glared at her sister and the group hooted and hollered.

"Lance and I are not a couple. Can we please get

back to Mandy's story, please?" Daisy objected, grabbing a Diet Dr. Pepper from the cooler.

"Okay, okay. So, obviously, Garrett is a doctor. Well, I had an appointment with a doctor in his office." Mandy looked around as everyone waited for the rest. "But I fell asleep and no one ever came to do my appointment."

"The doctor never came?" Poppy's mouth fell open with a laugh. "How long were you there?"

Mandy chuckled, "I'm not sure. I was pretty out of it. I think I woke up around eight that night? All I know is it was well after closing time, and Garrett thought I was an intruder. So not too far off from your story, Charlotte!"

Later in the evening, the women grew quieter. The sound of crickets and the cracking of the fire was interrupted occasionally by conversation. Poppy added another log to the fire. Somehow, she'd become the official firekeeper. Then she tipped her head back and studied the stars, taking in a deep breath of the smoke-scented air. Bloom's Farm was her favorite place on earth. Losing it was unimaginable. What would she do if she wasn't a farmer?

"Mandy, what would you do if you didn't run a daycare?"

The question broke the comfortable silence and

the women took turns answering the hypothetical question with their dream jobs or backup careers.

"If I didn't have the farm, I'd probably work at a veterinary clinic like I did in school," Poppy's youngest sister, Rose, offered. "Although, it's way more fun to do this than it is to give puppies their shots."

Chrissy chimed in, "If I didn't own the restaurant, I'd love to do something that involved travel. Like maybe write one of the travel memoirs I read."

"I'm already on my backup plan," Daisy said. "I couldn't be a professional dancer, so I decided to open a bed-and-breakfast. What about you, Poppy?"

"If I didn't have the farm?" Poppy considered. "I don't know. Maybe some sort of teacher?"

Snorts of laughter escaped from Lavender. "Come on, Poppy. There is no way you could be a teacher. You'd expel half your class before the first week was over."

"Yeah, maybe you could be a food blogger!" Danielle offered. "You know more about food than most people I met at culinary school." Danielle ran the bakery in Minden after moving from California last year.

Charlotte tapped a finger on her chin, "Hmm. You've got the whole activist vibe, Poppy. I think you would be a lobbyist for the Produce Growers of America or something." Poppy smiled at the nonexistent organization.

"Yeah, right. Politics? Not for me." Poppy insisted. From what she knew of Charlotte, the woman had an amazing ability to read people. Someone needed to speak up for small farms across America, but it definitely wasn't Poppy. No one listened to her around here; she would make a terrible activist.

The following Tuesday, Poppy took the four-wheeler to the orchard. The trampled pasture was the only evidence hundreds of people had visited the farm. Apple Days were over and she needed to see what remained on the trees. Then she needed to prep the fertilizer for the squash and pumpkins. It was time for their second application, and it seemed hard to believe it was nearly October.

Some in her family might call her obsessed with sustainable lifestyle, but Poppy simply embraced the benefits of fewer chemicals in her body. Her only brother, Hawthorne, claimed it made her a hippie. Over the years, she'd given up and embraced the label; at least within the family.

Poppy climbed down from the four-wheeler to duck between trees and take a better look at the inner rows, where people were unlikely to have picked apples. Judging by the trees she'd seen so far, there would be plenty to include a bag in the CSA boxes, plus making more apple butter. Maybe Danielle's bakery in Minden would be interested in offering it. She'd be sure to call her about it next week. Her phone vibrated and she glanced at the unfamiliar number before answering. Indianapolis.

"This is Poppy Bloom."

"I have Senator Coulter for you. Please hold."

Poppy frowned. This had to be a joke. First, there was no way Senator Coulter was calling her. Second, even if he were, surely he wouldn't have his assistant make the connection for him. She waited until a deep voice sounded in her ear. "Poppy, this is Harris–"

Poppy punched the red button with her thumb and slid her phone back into her pocket.

Twenty minutes and three ignored phone calls later, Poppy let her curiosity get the better of her when she saw a text message arrive. **Please talk to me.**

Was he kidding? Harrison Coulter, her friend and first love—unrequited love—was now a bigshot lawyer and state senator. His calling meant nothing good. Still, it had been five years since she had seen him at the Southwest Indiana Farm Association banquet in Terre Haute with a slinky blonde reporter on his arm. Since then, Poppy did her best to avoid events where he might be present, or even read news articles where he might be mentioned. Which was difficult, because he managed to insert himself into nearly every farm-related issue that came up in the state legislature. If she found out he was supporting The Farm Business Act, she would egg his office.

As though he could feel her weakening resolve, Harrison's number flashed on her screen again. Incoming call.

This time, instead of hitting ignore, Poppy hit the green button and held the phone to her ear, not speaking. "Poppy?" At least he hadn't made his secretary dial the number this time. She didn't answer. "At least let me know if you are there."

Poppy rolled her eyes and responded, "I'm here."

A sigh of relief sounded in her ear, "Thank you. I was really hoping to talk with you about something." He paused, as though waiting for her to respond. When she didn't, he continued, "This was a bad idea." Poppy could picture him, sitting at an enormous desk, probably in an expensive suit, rifling his fingers through his short brown hair. "Never mind,

Poppy. Forget I called." He sighed again and Poppy heard the defeat in his voice. What was going on? Why had he called her, and why did her heart automatically want to make it better? Something was bothering him, and she instinctively wanted to help. Too many years as friends could do that to a girl, even after a promise to leave him where he belonged —in the past.

"Harrison, wait." Poppy took a deep breath and asked herself if she was sure. She continued, "What do you want?"

Harrison groaned. "I need a date."

Poppy's eyes widened. "What? Did you say a date?"

Harrison continued, "Yeah, a date. Well, not just a date. I have something I needed to talk to you about. I thought maybe a date would give us a place to start."

Poppy narrowed her eyes, still unconvinced that someone wasn't playing a joke on her. Her brother, Hawthorne, was ornery like that. "Harrison?"

"Yes?"

"Is this really you?" He laughed and the sound sent vibrations rumbling all the way to her toes. Yep, that answered the question. No one else had ever had that impact on her.

"Okay, just making sure it was really you before I did this." Poppy hung up and slid the phone back into her pocket. Whatever had prompted Harrison to call her was something she wanted no part in. She'd forgiven him when he canceled their agreement to attend prom 'as friends' so he could take Melanie Crocker. She'd even forgiven him for the last-minute cancelation when he was supposed to visit her at Indiana University. But when he had promised to meet her in Indianapolis for her 20th birthday dinner and never showed? Poppy decided she would never waste her time pining away for Harrison Coulter.

Even if he begged her or promised her the world.

Still, she couldn't help but worry about The Farm Business Act being introduced to the senate in January. Harrison would undoubtedly be right in the middle of the discussion. Was he one of the senators being bought by the big farm corporations? It didn't seem like the Harrison she knew. But it had been almost twelve years since college. She had to face the reality that she didn't know him at all.

2

Two weeks later, Harrison was once again in Indianapolis for meetings, preparing for the busy holiday season, and the start of the legislative session after the New Year.

Neil sat across from him, once again sending not-so-subtle nudges that Harrison needed to find a wife. "Our initial poll numbers look promising. And when we ask sample voters their opinion of you if you were married, the numbers only get better." Neil gave a pointed look. "We even asked voters their opinions on a few potential matches, if you are curious."

Harrison's stomach roiled in disgust. The idea of choosing a wife based on the polling numbers was awful. What counted in those things? Did blondes poll better than brunettes? Or would someone with glasses make his wife seem smarter? Getting married to improve his chances was bad enough, but choosing one woman over another like that? He was not going that far.

He rolled his eyes and tried to distract his good friend with another topic, "Who are the other potential candidates for governor?"

With that, Neil rose and paced around the room. "It's still really early, but rumors around the capital make it seem like the field is pretty open. Of course you've got Senator Gilbert. He's a threat, but unlikeable as a crocodile. With his district being near Chicago, I think it would be difficult for the rest of the state to embrace him." As Neil continued to discuss the merits and downfalls of the various candidates, Harrison's mind wandered back to the problem at hand.

Harrison tried to name potential women, but the only one he could see working was Poppy. His ex-girlfriend, Stacy, would probably jump at the chance. But the idea of actually being married to Stacy made him shudder. Once upon a time, he thought he loved her. Now, Harrison was just thankful he had dodged that bullet. It was far easier to keep people at arm's length. When people got to know him, they inevitably decided he wasn't worth their loyalty or love. Appearances were all that mattered—his parents had taught him that. When Stacy had cheated on him, he'd been heartbroken, but her crocodile tears and staged apologies were too little, too late. He'd let Stacy in, and she eventually used that closeness as a weapon in her arsenal against him. It had been a significant wake-up call, and Harrison would rather be single forever than let someone else get close.

Neil had been texting him names of women they knew, and while some were perfectly nice, none had the personal connection he'd always had with Poppy. They'd been friends once. It seemed wise to at least base a marriage on friendship if you couldn't base it on romantic love. And Harrison wasn't going to fall in love with anyone. He'd tried that once and it only left you vulnerable. If he was going to be strong and a good leader, he needed to keep his head clear. A lifetime partnership with a friend for the betterment of society and to answer God's call together? That, he could do. Except, Harrison didn't really even have female friends, either.

Was it dishonest to not marry for love? Strategically, it would be best for the public to assume he did, probably a whirlwind romance ending in a short engagement. People all over the world married for other reasons, though. Arranged marriages, family alliances, or business deals. Why did it feel so transactional to do the same thing here?

Maybe that was why he was so adamant Poppy was the one. If she agreed, they would be in it together. Friends. Husband and Wife. But first, he had to convince her he wasn't a crazy, power-seeking louse.

At his surprisingly drab and depressing office provided in the State's capital, Harrison fingered the ivory invitation in his hand. The Indiana Organic and Sustainable Farming Association cordially invites you to The IOSFA 10th annual Harvest Gala.

Since becoming a state senator, Harrison had attended more benefits, galas, and awards banquets than he ever knew existed. Most were unimportant, not warranting more than a kind note with a Decline RSVP. If he actually attended, they were barely tolerable even if they were for a good cause. In his most charitable mood, these events grated his nerves. Being stuck in a stuffy ballroom in his suit, or worse, his tuxedo, was not his idea of public service. Occasionally, he could justify skipping an event, often scheduling his trips back to Terre Haute strategically in order to decline without offense. But this particular event, when it crossed his desk, gave him an idea.

Harrison punched a button on his phone that connected him to Bethany's phone. "Don't you add a pile of work on me today, Senator. I've got a mani-pedi at four o'clock."

He smiled. Bethany got more done before nine this morning than he would accomplish all day. "I just need you to work some of that Bethany magic for me. I need to know more about the Indiana Organic and Sustainable Farming Association."

"The Indiana who what Association?"

"I've got the invite in here. I'm curious about their membership. Think you can dig anything up?"

"Hmm. I'll see what I can do. No promises." Bethany hung up on him, and he fingered the invitation. She might not make promises, but Bethany had this town wired. If anyone could get the information, it was the vivacious gray-haired woman with loyal friends scattered throughout Indiana's political system.

If Poppy was still the same girl he knew so many years ago, there was nothing she cared more for than her family and her family farm. In fact, it wasn't just *her* farm that Poppy was passionate about. It was farming in general and the success of smaller, more sustainable operations. An event from an organization specifically created with a mission that aligned with her philosophy exactly was more than an event on his calendar. This was an opportunity. If he could convince Poppy to attend the event with him, maybe it would give him a chance to see where things stood between them. She'd hung up on him twice last week and balked at the mention of a date. If that didn't bring his ego down a notch, he didn't know what would. But maybe if it were for the greater good, she'd consider it.

They were close once, a long time ago. They went from being friends to barely speaking, in his mind because of attending different colleges. He winced. There had been the time he canceled his visit. And the time he forgot about meeting her in Indianapolis. After that, Poppy let him have it and completely cut off contact with him.

No wonder she thought so little of him. Young and cocky at the time, Harrison had brushed off her anger; it was her loss. Now, he wondered if that was true. He didn't meet women like Poppy Bloom every day. The women in his circles these days were ambitious and conniving. They saw him as a path to their own success, not as a person. It was becoming more and more difficult to find a woman who shared the convictions he held about faith and family. If he were friends with Poppy today, he would definitely be less selfish than the twenty-year-old version of himself. And he would never have let her sit in a restaurant alone waiting for him.

Harrison dialed Poppy's number, hoping she would answer.

When the line went to voicemail, he left a message, "Hi Poppy, this is Senator Coulter." Great, way to keep it casual. "Sorry, this is Harrison. I know you hate me. Can you just... call me back? Please?" Harrison wasn't usually so awkward and self-conscious, and he never begged people to call him. But Poppy? She was different. The more he prayed about governorship, the more he was convinced it was the move he needed to make. If Neil was convinced that Harrison needed a woman by his side to run this state, then Harrison would do it. Now, he just had to convince Poppy that she wanted it, too. Before Harrison could consider it at length, his office phone rang, and his administrative assistant reminded him that a meeting was due to start in ten minutes.

Later that night, as Harrison wandered the stark, modern apartment he kept in Indianapolis, his thoughts drifted back to the last time he had seen Poppy.

He walked into the Southwest Indiana Farm Association banquet in Terre Haute with Stacy on his arm, her high-pitched whine grating on his nerves. "I don't see why they couldn't host this at someplace nicer than the Holiday Inn. I mean, honestly, there are people here in jeans, Harry." Harrison studied his own dark gray suit and button-down shirt, only slightly overdressed compared to the farmers and agriculture professionals scattered through the room in khakis and dress shirts.

Neil walked over, "Harrison, I'm glad you made it. I've said it before and I'll say it again—you've got to embrace your country roots and show this state you value the farm economy. These guys will love you." Neil glanced to Stacy, "Hi, Stacy. Nice to see you again." His tone was less-than friendly, and Harrison gave him a look of warning.

"Harry, can you go get me a glass of champagne?" Harrison hated being called Harry, but he loved Stacy. Sometimes.

"Wine and beer only," Neil chimed in, raising his own dark-amber bottle.

Stacy rolled her eyes in disgust. "Ugh, fine. White wine, then. Thanks, sweetie."

Harrison extracted himself from his girlfriend and headed toward the bar. As he grew closer, a familiar laugh caught his ear and he searched until he found her. Poppy was in the midst of a lively discussion, surrounded on all sides by men twenty-five years older than her. They laughed, reacting to something she said.

At one point, Poppy looked up as though sensing his eyes upon her, and her mouth fell open. Her expression could have been one of surprise or regret, but as quickly as it flashed, it was gone. Poppy looked away, smiled warmly at one of the men and tucked an errant strand of auburn hair behind her ear.

Harrison stepped to the outskirts of the circle. He watched, amazed at the confidence of his old friend. It was clear Poppy already knew these men, and she was as much a part of their circle as he was not.

"Come on, Roger. We just put up a new greenhouse at Bloom's Farm. I'm telling you, I'm going to have fresh, ripe tomatoes for your wife in March so she can make you a BLT that will have you itching for a summer picnic." Gracefully, Poppy pulled Harrison into the conversation, "What do you think, Senator? Is Community-Supported Agriculture a sustainable business strategy?" Harrison put on his best politician smile and began charming the farmers, finding connections with his family and directing the conversation exactly where he was most comfortable. Before he knew it, Poppy had ducked away and disappeared.

His phone rang, pulling him back to the present, and when he answered, Poppy's voice rang clearly across the line.

"Hey, it's Poppy. You left a message?" She sounded curious, but cold. He missed being able to make her laugh.

"How was your day?" He looked up at the ceiling and pressed his palm against his forehead. Lame question, Senator.

"It was fine." At least she hadn't hung up. Poppy continued, and Harrison leaned on the countertop of the spotless kitchen he never used. "This time of year is easier for me. We don't plant as many fall crops, and almost everything else is already harvested. I'll be ready for Halloween and Thanksgiving to be over." Poppy paused before blurting, "Why did you call?"

Okay, so much for small talk. "I received an invitation to the IOSFA Harvest Gala happening next week." He had received invitations in the past but never attended. As far as he knew, neither had any of his legislative colleagues. As far as events went—even within the world of agriculture—this was not a high-profile one. But he had a gut feeling it would be something Poppy might be involved in.

Bethany had called in a favor and gotten the membership roster from the organization. It was small, but growing. One name in particular caught his eye. Poppy Bloom, member for five years. "Will you be there?"

"I wasn't planning on it," she sounded confused.

"Oh, that's too bad. I was considering attending if it meant I would see you."

"Really?" She sounded skeptical, and Harrison's conscience twinged. This was manipulative, and he didn't like it. But what was his other option? He needed to see Poppy to see if there was any chance for a future.

"Well, you should still go. It would mean so much to the IOSFA to have you there." The excitement in her voice confirmed his suspicions. Poppy cared about the organization; this was his leverage.

"I don't know, Poppy. I really am quite busy. And you know how I dread these types of events. Maybe if I knew there would be a familiar face..." He trailed off, his insinuation clear.

"Are you saying you will attend the event if I go?" Leave it to Poppy to cut to the chase.

"That is what I am saying."

"That is kind of dirty, isn't it, Coulter?" She was right, it was, but he had to do it. To make himself feel better, Harrison committed to attending the event even if she turned him down.

"Will you go with me?"

Poppy sighed, "Why are you doing this?"

"Does it matter? Don't you want the IOSFA to be successful?" It was a low blow, even Harrison knew that. Before she could call him on it, like he knew she would, he continued, "Look, it's just dinner. One you will have way more fun at than I will. And if you agree to come, I will attend, and my office will issue a press release about my support for the organization and my attendance at the event." Poppy was quiet for a moment, and he knew he had her. Come on, say yes.

"This weekend?" Harrison confirmed and smiled when she agreed to go.

"Awesome. My assistant will be in touch. I will pick you up at your hotel for the event." Poppy stammered, and Harrison ignored it. "See you soon, Poppy."

3

After the call, Poppy laid on her bed for a long time.

What on earth just happened? How had Harrison known she was a supporter of the IOSFA? Regardless, she should have said no. The organization had existed for decades without the presence of the oh-so-important Senator Coulter. Still, they'd been struggling with getting their message out. If Harrison came to the event, maybe other bigwigs would, too. That would be huge for them. Poppy wasn't on the board of directors right now, but she still cared. The IOSFA had been a huge help to Bloom's Farm when they made the switch to organic and sustainable farming, providing resources and information, plus a grant for marketing expenses.

Poppy wanted them to succeed, and now it meant putting up with Harrison Coulter for the evening. Or being in the same room with him, at least. No matter what he said, there was no way he was treating this like a date! She would meet him at the dinner, shake his hand, and introduce him to her friends from around the state. Poppy would make sure her table was full and Harrison happened to be seated in the very back, preferably behind a support column where she couldn't see him even if she wanted to.

She did want to find out what he knew about The Farm Business Act. Maybe try to sway his decision by reminding him of the importance of small, local farms. She frowned; that conversation would mean more time talking to Harrison at the Harvest Gala. If it meant saving her farm and hundreds of others, surely she could put up with his ego and campaign-ad smile for one evening. Poppy couldn't let anyone know, though. She would never hear the end of it from Daisy or Lavender, which meant keeping her trip to Indianapolis quiet for a while.

No one would notice if she were gone for one night, but she needed to make sure the farm was taken care of. The next day, she called Hawthorne and asked him to take a look at the tractor tires. They were probably due to be replaced, but maybe he could inspect them and make sure they were still safe. While he was working, she came by to talk to him. She twisted her rings around her fingers, trying to figure out how to ask the favor she needed. Hawthorne was her best bet of getting away from the farm without a full-on interrogation.

Glancing up from the tractor tire he was inspecting, Hawthorne raised an eyebrow. "Spill it, Poppy."

Poppy released her hands and took a breath before letting it out. "I need to get away for a day or two."

Hawthorne stood and grabbed a rag to wipe his hands. "For what?" Her brother's tone was casual, but those two simple words carried concern and care. Her brother really was sweeter than they gave him credit for. Hopefully Avery would see that soon.

Poppy looked down to avoid the questions in his eyes, "I can't say. But I need someone to keep an eye on things for me." She looked up at him, almost a full head taller. "Lewis and Clint know everything that needs done, but if anything happens... Could you just run things around here for a few days?"

Hawthorne frowned. "What about Dad?" he asked.

Poppy's shoulders sagged. "I was hoping not to bring Mom and Dad into this." Her farmhands would be fine. She should have just let them know and then disappeared. They had her cell phone. She turned away, her cotton skirt twirling around her boots. "It's fine. Forget I asked."

Hawthorne spoke up as she walked away, "Wait, wait. I'll do it."

She turned back toward him with a sigh of relief. Hawthorne held up a finger, "But you owe me. And I expect to hear what this is all about sooner rather than later," he gave her a pointed look. She nodded with a smile and Hawthorne's eyes widened, "You're not eloping with some guy, right?"

Poppy scoffed at him, "Who would I run away with? You know I haven't been seeing anyone." Then, she stepped in close and wrapped her arms around him. He held the dirty rag away from her and patted her shoulder. "Thanks, Hawthorne."

"Yeah, yeah. Just be careful with whatever you're doing."

Typical Hawthorne to be concerned and protective. But it was one event. Poppy tracked her farmhands down checking on the last of the pumpkins and winter squash. After letting them know

Hawthorne would be their main contact for the next few days, Poppy went back to the main house to pack a bag.

The night of the event, Poppy stood in the elegantly decorated hotel suite in the heart of downtown Indianapolis. When Harrison's assistant had called, Poppy tried every trick in the book to change the plan and simply meet Harrison at the event. His assistant was apparently very good at her job, and before Poppy even knew what happened, she had agreed to let Harrison handle all the arrangements for her visit to the capital.

There was a garment bag hanging on the closet door. She had definitely not agreed to this. Still, curiosity beckoned, and Poppy was only human. She unzipped the bag and gasped at the sight of a gorgeous satin evening dress. The cost of this dress could probably buy her a new tractor. Okay, maybe not. It would at least cover new tires for the one she had. Poppy fingered the deep midnight blue fabric wistfully. What was Harrison up to? Giving the stunning gown one last glance, she made her way to the bedroom to change into her own dress. Harrison may like to control every situation, but he had no claim on her. He'd given that up twelve years ago.

She might want to support the IOSFA, but Poppy had only agreed to attend the event, not be his personal Barbie doll.

Poppy finished her makeup and braided her hair into a simple style that left her hair trailing across her collarbone. Pleased with the final image, Poppy narrowed her eyes at her reflection. Harrison Coulter could eat his heart out.

A knock sounded at her hotel door, and Poppy took a deep breath to steel her nerves, smoothing nonexistent wrinkles from the front of her dress. Opening the door, she was greeted by the unfairly gorgeous sight of Harrison Coulter in a tailored suit and white dress shirt. In his hand, he held a single rose, as though he were the contestant on a cheesy reality dating show. I would watch that, she mused. Harrison's eyes flickered over her dress and his eyes danced in amusement. He handed her the rose, "This is for you. You look lovely." Then Harrison took two ties from his pocket. One was the exact color of the dress stilling hanging on the closet door. He tucked it in his pocket with a chuckle, "I thought I might need a backup plan. A man can hope, right?" He glanced inside the hotel room and held up his tie. "May I?"

Speechless, Poppy stepped aside and waved him into her room so he could use the mirror. He was prepared for anything, wasn't he? The fact that Harrison knew her well enough to recognize that she was unlikely to appreciate his wardrobe suggestion made her stomach feel tingly and light. This was not supposed to be fun. Unable to resist, she buried her nose in the sweet petals of the floribunda rose. She knew this variety was grown to be especially fragrant. Did Harrison know that? She inhaled the sweet aroma, averting her eyes to avoid watching the delectable sight of Harrison Coulter swiftly knotting his tie, a perfectly unobtrusive gray and white pattern that neither matched nor clashed with the floral evening dress she wore.

His usually short hair was a touch too long, as though he hadn't had time to visit the barber, and his tan skin and clean-shaved jaw line taunted her with familiarity. This was the same boy she'd loved ten years ago, but he was also older, stronger. And, if possible, more handsome. Coulter had grown taller, another inch or two since high school, and his shoulders filled out the tailored suit far better than he had in high school.

Poppy closed her eyes, focusing on the rose and repeating her mantra for the evening. This was not supposed to be fun. This was not a date, she reminded herself. Poppy laid the flower on the bedspread and grabbed a small clutch she had secretly borrowed from Lavender. When Harrison held out his arm, she ignored it and opened the door for herself. This would be a long night.

4

Poppy climbed out when Harrison opened the car door. He ushered her inside as the valet took his car, a black sedan with surprisingly soft leather seats. He'd come a long way from the loud farm truck he'd driven in high school. Harrison's family always had money, and it had been easy to forget when they were in school. But now? She still drove a rattily old farm truck, and he drove back and forth from his law office in Terre Haute to his senatorial office in Indianapolis in sheer luxury.

Their differences seemed even more evident at the dinner. The Harvest Gala was being held at the JW Marriott in downtown Indianapolis. Even though the IOSFA were Poppy's peers, there were far more politicians, philanthropists, and Indianapolis socialites than she expected. Which was great for the organization and not so reassuring for Poppy.

As they entered the ballroom, Harrison was greeted warmly by someone she didn't recognize.

"Harrison, so good to see you!" The middle-aged man, fit and well-dressed, greeted Harrison with a firm handshake, clasping his upper arm before turning his eyes to Poppy. "And who is this enchanting creature you've brought with you?" The man's eyes twinkled with mischief and kindness.

Harrison flashed her one of his signature grins. "Well, actually, she brought me. This is Poppy Bloom, an old friend. Her passion for organic farming methods is the reason I am here tonight. Poppy, this is Judge Aarons, from the 7th circuit court of appeals."

"Nice to meet you, Your Honor." Poppy held out her hand.

"The pleasure is mine, Miss Bloom. Call me Frank. When I mentioned to Harrison last week that I was looking for a way to support local farms like the one I grew up on, he pointed me to this event."

Poppy glanced at the man standing next to her, amazed at his dedication to whatever this night meant for him. He was really trying to win her over.

"It should be a wonderful evening," Poppy responded. It seemed like the safest response.

"Save me a dance, Miss Bloom? I'd love to talk to a woman who knows as much as you do about the future of local farms." Frank gave a friendly smile, and Poppy's couldn't help but return one of her own. Harrison's judge friend wasn't so bad.

They continued into the ballroom, making introductions when people stopped to chat. Harrison was deep in conversation with the local restauranteur, and Poppy tuned out, scanning the room. The organizers had gone all out, with beautiful harvest cornucopias on the tables. Pumpkins, gourds, sunflowers and calico corncobs spilled elegantly onto gold tablecloths. Soft candles and ambient lighting gave the room a warm, cozy feel despite the large space and crowd.

As she studied the room and absently fingered the fabric of Harrison's suit, Poppy spotted the last person she hoped to see. The blond toothpick-in-a-dress strutted toward Harrison, her eyes narrowing at the sight of Poppy on his arm. Refusing to be intimidated, Poppy tightened her grip on Harrison's elbow.

"Well, if it isn't my Harry!" Stacy squealed from three tables away. Poppy choked at the nickname; Harrison *hated* being called Harry. The muscles of

Harrison's arm flexed under her hand. "I had *no idea* you were going to be here!" To her left, Harrison quickly ended the conversation and turned toward the shrill voice quickly approaching them.

"I find that hard to believe, Stacy. You know, since there was a press release and all."

Stacy waved a hand, "Pfft. You know I don't follow the news."

"Aren't you a reporter?" Poppy asked. Harrison coughed to cover a laugh.

Stacy's eyes flashed, "I am a news anchor, thank you very much. And you would be...?"

Poppy gave a broad smile. "Poppy Bloom. Farmer." She offered her hand and tried not to show her horror when Stacy held her hand up limply, palm down, as though Poppy should kiss her ring. She shook it awkwardly and released it as soon as possible. What was wrong with this woman?

"A farmer!" Stacy repeated. "How...quaint." The condescension dripped from Stacey's words and Poppy wanted to go back in time to have Andi teach her hand-to-hand combat. With her sister's ninja moves, Poppy could ruin Stacy's perfectly arranged face with maximum efficiency.

Stacy reached for Harrison with manicured fingers, expertly adjusting the color-coordinated pocket square he wore. Jealousy raged, just like it had years ago when Poppy watched Stacy cling to Harrison's arm at the dinner in Terre Haute. It shouldn't bother her that Stacy still wanted Harrison. This was not a date. Repeat: not a date!

Poppy cleared her throat and turned to Harrison, ignoring the way his eyes were glued to Stacy's hands on his pocket. "Should we go find our table, *Harry*?" His eyes moved to Poppy's, and she saw the storm clouds gathered in them. But was it desire for Stacy? Or irritation? Anger?

Then Stacy interjected, "Shouldn't you be harvesting or something, Penny?"

Oh well, inefficient methods of ripping Stacy's face off would work just fine. Poppy tensed and Harrison stepped close, laying a hand on hers before ducking close to whisper in her ear, "Don't let her get to you, Poppy." Her breath caught as his cheek brushed her jawline. Then it was gone, and Stacy's fingers moved to fix his tie as Poppy watched in disbelief.

Harrison stepped out of Stacy's reach, desperate to have her polished talons off his suit. Poppy's reaction to his ex-girlfriend was interesting, though. As much as he would like to see the feisty attitude he remembered, it wouldn't be a great start to his potential campaign. He turned to Poppy, amused at the jealous glare she was sending Stacy, "Why don't you find our table and I will be right there." It was time to end Stacy's fixation with him, once and for all.

Poppy gave him a confused look, and he flashed what he hoped was a reassuring smile. Her fingers trailed away, and he longed for the contact to return immediately after they were gone.

Stacy flashed a victorious smile toward Poppy as she walked away, "I'm sure you'll see him later, Polly." Harrison jaw clenched at Stacy's disrespect.

Harrison gestured to the exit, inviting Stacy to follow him out of the ballroom. Instead of walking ahead of him, she clung to the empty crook of his elbow Poppy had held only moments before. Trying not to grimace in disgust, he walked her quickly to the exit. Safely in the hallway, he extricated his arm from her two-handed grasp and stepped several feet away.

A pout crossed Stacy's features, the hurt evident in her eyes. Ack, why did he feel guilty? She was the one who had cheated on him, used him for his political connections, and was cruel and judgmental.

Still, he thought he loved her once, and they had shared a lot of time before he recognized her true colors.

He rubbed a hand across his jaw, “Stacy,” he started.

“I've got a room upstairs,” she said, rolling her shoulders seductively and flashing a suggestive smile. “Farmer Jane will be fine.”

His stomach rolled in disgust. While dating Stacy, Harrison had been tempted to compromise his faith, and her pressure to take things further physically had tormented him. But now, her invitation held no appeal. “What? No, Stacy—”

“Harrison,” she whined, “Haven't you punished me enough? It wasn't my fault, Harry, I swear!” Stacy stepped close, her hands on him again.

His frustration simmered and Harrison once again stepped away. “Not your fault, Stacy? Are you crazy?” He threw his hands in the air. “Of course you are. Look,” he held up a hand to stop her in her tracks as she came toward him again, “Leave. Me. Alone. We are not together. We will never be together. I am with Poppy, and if I find out you have done anything to jeopardize our relationship, I will make sure you never work anything beyond the early morning local news slot you have now. Got it?” He was practically shaking with anger and desperate to return to Poppy's side inside the ballroom. Harrison might have stretched the truth with the whole *I am with Poppy* line, but it was true tonight anyway.

Without waiting for a response, he pulled his suit jacket down and rolled his neck to relieve the tension in his muscles before walking back into the dimly lit ballroom.

If he never saw Stacy Adler again, it would be too soon. Now he had to go find Poppy and try to convince her to marry him. No sweat.

Poppy sat alone at an elegantly decorated table, stewing over Harrison's absence. Where had he disappeared to with that deranged barbie doll? Poppy looked around, trying to find a friendly face, but somehow, all she saw were unfamiliar men in suits and classy-looking women in evening gowns worth more than her truck. Where were her IOSFA people?

A hand landed on her bare shoulder and she jumped. When Poppy turned, she was greeted by the smiling face of Andrew Treat. Standing, she embraced him with a warm hug. "Andrew! How are you? Is Lisha here?" she glanced around, hoping to see his wife. When Poppy had considered transitioning Bloom's farm from a simple two crop operation, Andrew and Lisha had opened their farm and home to her for three weeks to help her learn.

Andrew's eyes brightened at the mention of his wife, but he shook his head. "Actually, Lisha is resting at home. It's still not common knowledge, but come next Harvest season, we'll have another little Treat around the farm keeping us busy!"

Poppy hugged him again, "Congratulations! What is that, number three?"

Andrew beamed, "Four actually."

"That's wonderful. I'm so happy for you." Andrew and Lisha were the same age as Poppy but had married in college. Now they had four kids! Poppy was starting to think she would never have that experience. She was so busy with the farm, and the only men she really saw often were her father, Hawthorne, Clint, and Lewis. Of course, her two farmhands were both her father's age.

While she asked questions about the due date and how the big brothers and sister were handling the news, Poppy felt the familiar awareness that Harrison drew near. Her body had built-in Harrison radar, and it was apparently well-tuned despite the years since it had been activated. He appeared to her right, his politician smile pasted in place.

Poppy called this surface-level, polite smile his politician smile. It wasn't the same one he used to give her, or even the one she saw him give to Judge Aarons. Harrison's politician smile was kind and obviously won the hearts of many, but it didn't compare to his heartfelt grin. That genuine smile could make her knees give out.

"Hello, I'm Harrison Coulter. You must be a friend of Poppy's." Harrison slipped a territorial hand around Poppy's waist, and she fought the urge to step further into his embrace. Instead, she increased the distance between them and lectured herself for wanting more contact. This was for IOSFA. Harrison extended a hand to Andrew, and the young farmer gave her a wide-eyed look. Poppy fidgeted uncomfortably as heat rose in her cheeks. Andrew would have far too many questions after this.

Andrew introduced himself and made small talk with Harrison. Harrison's smile brightened when Andrew mentioned his wife and kids, and he became much friendlier. This was ridiculous. Her own flash of jealousy at Stacy's presence was bad enough. Harrison had no right to expect her to fall at his feet.

He had broken her heart and trust and didn't even know it. Now, he just showed up out of nowhere and started acting like they are together.

She stepped further away, forcing Harrison to remove his hand. No matter how good it felt, Poppy refused to let herself fall for Harrison again. It could only lead to heartbreak. She needed him to help save the farm. Beyond that, he could find other dates for his future events.

5

Poppy survived the rest of the evening, conveniently distracting Harrison with people to meet each time they almost had time for actual conversation. He had been irritated when she insisted on calling her own cab, thanking him for the evening and rushing away without giving him a chance to object. Poppy was too afraid a conversation in the dark, quiet of his car would be too much to handle. Instead, she retreated to the private hide-away of her hotel room.

Since she'd come home, he was no less persistent. A few text messages each day, asking how she was or thanking her for the evening. And at least one phone call.

Tired of ignoring him, Poppy finally answered

his call on her way to her office in the back of the pole-barn.

"You have to stop calling me," she stated flatly.

He chuckled. "That's just not true, Poppy. But if you'll just hear me out, I'll promise to follow your wishes."

She glanced around to make sure no one could hear her. "Harrison, I'm glad you went to the Harvest Gala. From what Andrew told me, it made a huge difference in their attendance and fundraising numbers. But that's all it was. One night."

"Come on. Didn't we have a good time?" Poppy fingered her braid. They did have a good time. Harrison was funny and polite—a perfect gentleman. They'd danced and talked about their families during dinner.

Still, his ego needed no stroking. "It was fine."

He laughed, as though he knew exactly what she was doing. "I had a great time, too. But there is something I need to talk to you about, and we never got the chance."

A four-wheeler pulled up outside the barn; her time was limited. "There's no need for us to meet. Whatever it is, the answer is no."

"Poppy, please."

A stream of light entered the barn as the door

opened. Daisy stepped inside and headed toward her. Trying to hide her words from her sister, Poppy turned toward the wall and lowered her voice. "This is not going to happen."

"I'll just keep bugging you until you agree."

Daisy was getting closer and Poppy's pulse kicked into overdrive. "Harrison, I can't—"

"I'll be in Terre Haute next week. Meet me then?"

Daisy was only a few feet away, and Poppy whispered, "Fine."

"Great, I'll text you the details." She heard the satisfaction in his voice and tipped her head back in frustration. She hung up without a farewell and smiled at her sister.

Daisy looked at the phone and frowned. "Who was that?" she asked.

Poppy played dumb, "Who was who?"

Daisy raised her eyebrow. Of course, her sister would be able to spot Poppy's lie. Daisy didn't push, but offered a listening shoulder if Poppy needed one.

Poppy nodded, "Thanks. It's just a bit... complicated right now."

Daisy scoffed and said, "Tell me about it. I've got cyberbullies and crawlspace kisses. Plus, Hawthorne is being all weird and responsible."

"Whoa, whoa, whoa. Crawlspace kisses?" She pushed Daisy over to a bench against the wall of the barn. "I'm going to need a bit more information than that." Maybe Poppy could get Daisy to talk and forget anything she might have heard.

But Daisy was relentless in her interrogation and refused to be distracted. Finally, wanting to share with someone, Poppy sighed and then gave a sheepish smile, "It's Harrison."

Daisy's mouth dropped open in shock, "Like, your Harrison? Harrison Coulter?"

Eyes squeezed shut, Poppy nodded quickly. She opened one eye to gauge Daisy's reaction.

"Oh my, what did he want?"

If only Poppy knew. "Sorry, that's all I can tell you right now."

"Are you kidding me? That's the biggest tease!" Her sister pushed a hand against Poppy's shoulder.

Poppy smiled. "I don't know... Crawlspace kisses is a pretty big teaser, too, Daze." Daisy blushed and Poppy knew she had her. Her contractor, Lance, had kissed her in the crawlspace. Plus, the bed and breakfast was the target of fake reviews online, and it wasn't even open yet. Daisy was struggling with how to respond; her sister's instinct was to fight back with everything she had.

Poppy patted her sister's shoulder. "Well, I don't think 'an eye for an eye' is a great strategy."

"I do hate that 'turn the other cheek' passage," Daisy frowned.

"Pray about it. Maybe God has something He is working out," Poppy offered. It was probably good advice for her to consider herself. For some reason, Harrison was intent on meeting with her. Maybe she just needed to pray about it and have an open mind.

"That's good advice." Daisy admitted. "Thanks."

"As for Lance—same advice," Poppy finished. "Pray about it. Maybe the answer will surprise you."

When Daisy left, Poppy jumped online for her usual check on the IOSFA message boards. Her counterparts at farms across the state used the forum to discuss everything from germination techniques to marketing strategies. These were her people. A new forum post caught her eye, the title making her heart race. An inside source at Senator Hawkins office.

Inside the discussion, Poppy's heart dropped when she read the poster's comments.

My cousin works in Senator Hawkins office and she called yesterday. According to her, the Farm Business Act is definitely Hawkins' number one priority during the upcoming session. He is already trading favors and working on his votes. From the snippets I could read in photos she sent of the planned bill, it could be truly horrendous for us. Has anyone else heard anything about this?

Poppy read through the rest of the comments, searching for anyone with a hint of good news. No one mentioned Harrison, but that didn't mean he wouldn't be involved. Was he trading favors for his vote?

The idea that someone could threaten her livelihood and make her feel so helpless against it made Poppy want to toss her keyboard. What was she supposed to do about a threat that came from a man of power and was backed by millions of dollars from corporate agriculture giants? If only she had the connections Harrison did, maybe she could make a difference. Walking through the IOSFA banquet, he seemed to know everyone. Of course, it helped that he came from three generations of Indiana royalty. His grandfather had been governor a long time ago, and his family still had enormous power in the state.

Poppy Bloom, though? She didn't have much power anywhere, except maybe when it came to the committee for the Minden farmer's market. They usually listened to her. She thought about her suggestion that they separate the craft and food booths. Carolyn Polaski and her handmade goat milk soap had quickly rallied the committee against that suggestion. But otherwise? Poppy had sway there. Of course, that was much different from convincing one-hundred state senators to vote against a bill that promised jobs and corporate tax revenue.

Depressed, Poppy closed her laptop and headed to the pumpkin field. She would have pie pumpkins and squash for the CSA baskets this week, but the decorative pumpkins needed to be picked and loaded up for the Minden Fall Festival. Her farmhands, Clint and Lewis, had been cutting pumpkins from the vines all morning and loading them in the back of the wagon. The festival was next week, but she and Hawthorne would go set up on Friday. She texted Lavender.

Don't forget. Next Saturday, festival in Minden. You agreed to help this year!

Lavender was the least outdoorsy of the Bloom siblings, followed closely by Lily who was always crisp and professional as she managed the event venue on the farm. Lavender was fashionable and shy, far more comfortable behind a screen than on a horse. Not that Poppy rode the horses much anymore. Four-wheelers were easier and less likely to get distracted by eating the long grass on the side of the gravel or dirt roads.

When she got to the patch, Poppy was unsurprised to see her dad working alongside Lewis and Clint, joking with his old friends.

She climbed out of her truck and walked towards the men. "Hey, Dad. Don't you think you should let someone else do that?"

In response, her father grabbed another pumpkin and lifted it into the trailer.

"We keep trying to tell him it's not a job for the elderly, but he's too stubborn." Lewis gave a hearty chuckle at his own joke. Poppy rolled her eyes. Truth was, Lewis was only two years younger than her father.

"Bah. It's good exercise. Besides, somebody needed to make sure these troublemakers were pulling their weight."

Poppy smiled. "Yeah, I keep telling Clint he is still on probation. When did we hire him, about fifteen years ago?"

"Nineteen years," Clint corrected, "You were only about yay-high back then," he held his hand to his waist, "and determined to work in the fields near as hard as your daddy."

Keith smiled and laughed, "She did always love driving the tractor."

"Got it stuck a time or two, if memory serves right."

Poppy held up a hand, "Okay, okay. Enough with the trip down memory lane. How much longer you guys think we got here?"

Poppy asked for forty pie pumpkins and eighty zucchini squash to be set inside the barn. She personally packed the CSA baskets each Friday before Clint and Lewis took them to the pick-up locations in Terre Haute and Greencastle. It was becoming more difficult to manage the growing produce business. Between the certification work for organic suppliers, the bi-weekly CSA baskets, and her normal farmers markets, Poppy had little time to spare.

She said goodbye to her farmhands and her father, then took the four-wheeler out to her favorite spot on the ranch. Poppy stepped down and began to walk through the empty grapevines she had planted five years ago. The winery was a fun side project, tucked in a corner of the property.

Two years ago, she had attempted her first batch of homemade wine with the grapes, and the harvest from this year was currently fermenting and would soon be ready to bottle. With everything else she had going on, it seemed silly to add more to her plate, but she'd taken a class on grapes and winemaking as part of her degree in agronomy horticulture and loved everything about it. Someday, the winery could be another part of a thriving Bloom's Farm, with a tasting room or the ability to offer Bloom's Farm wines to be served at events held at Storybook Barn and organized by her sister Lily.

For now though, the grapevines were empty, and though the grass was getting tall, there wasn't much to do out here but think. Even with no fruit on the vines, there was something relaxing about the orderly rows. Grapevines always reminded her of scripture, the countless places where God is referred to as the vine—the source. As long as she stayed connected to the vine, like her grapes, she would be just fine. She just had to remember that when she worried about things out of her control.

6

The following week, Poppy met Harrison in Terre Haute. She hadn't stopped thinking about what he might want to talk about. This whole situation was bizarre; they hadn't been close for years. Even before they both went off to college, their friendship was starting to fade away. It had been too hard for Poppy to remain friends with Harrison in light of her feelings for him since he obviously didn't see her the same way. To make matters worse, he chose to take someone else to prom 'on a real date' instead of keeping their agreement to go as friends. Standing her up for her 20th birthday in Indianapolis had been the last straw.

Her curiosity hadn't gotten the memo about giving up, though. Whatever Harrison wanted to talk about, it was obviously important to him. His schedule in Terre Haute was busy, based on the text messages they had exchanged trying to schedule this dinner. Still, he made it very clear that whatever worked for Poppy, he would make work for him.

Tempted to primp, Poppy instead showered after her daily work was finished and pulled her hair back into the braid she wore most days, spritzing with hairspray to tame the flyaways. Her rickety old farm truck felt wildly out of place at D'Armaggio's, the nicest restaurant in Terre Haute, parked next to expensive SUVs and sleek sedans. She found a spot at the back of the lot and pulled her cross-body bag over her shoulder before jumping down from the truck. The walk to the restaurant was cold, the frigid wind biting through her thin wool peacoat.

When she pulled open the heavy wooden door of the restaurant, the warm blast of garlic-laden air welcomed her inside. It was heavenly. Poppy closed her eyes and drank in the scent of fresh bread and spices. When she opened them, she spotted Harrison leaning confidently against the wall of the entryway. Even in an upscale restaurant, he seemed a step above the rest of the dressed-up couples waiting on the cushioned benches.

Harrison smirked at her obvious appreciation,

and she felt her cheeks burn. He straightened and waved a finger at the hostess, who gave him a shy smile, pulled two menus from her stack, and gestured him to follow her. Of course Harrison would never have to wait for a table. He held his hand out for her to hold as they followed the waitress silently. It felt a little bit like a walk to the gallows, following her executioner.

Harrison helped Poppy out of her coat, handing it discretely to the hostess, then held out her chair and pushed it in under her as she sat. He sat across from her, unbuttoning his suit jacket as he did so.

"You look lovely tonight, Poppy," he said softly. Their table was small, tucked in the corner of the restaurant with far too much privacy for her liking. She knew not a single other person could hear his words; they were only for her.

"Thank you."

"Would you like a glass of wine?" he asked.

Poppy declined. The last thing she needed was to lower her inhibitions around the Most Eligible Bachelor in Indiana.

"Thanks for agreeing to have dinner. We have some things to discuss," he added.

Poppy frowned, "Like what? What is this all about?"

Harrison smiled tightly. "Let's just eat and I'll explain the whole thing. What sounds good?"

Frustrated and impatient, Poppy sighed and picked up her menu. If he was making this a whole big thing, she was at least going to enjoy her dinner. The upscale restaurant wasn't exactly on her frequently visited restaurant list, but the food was excellent.

The waitress appeared silently next to the table, "Welcome to D'Armaggio's, Senator. It is our pleasure to have you dining with us tonight. Can I get you anything to drink or an appetizer perhaps?"

Harrison ordered a starter and iced tea for both of them. After the server was gone, Poppy tried to remember if the young woman had looked at her even once. Maybe that was why Harrison couldn't find a girlfriend. He would always be the center of attention, which for some women, would be frustrating. Of course, for Poppy, who'd grown up with the chaos of seven kids around, she was used to being overlooked.

Harrison offered Poppy the breadbasket and she took a piece, pulling small pieces off and nibbling on them.

"Are you ready for the Harvest Festival over in Minden? Isn't that coming up soon?"

Poppy smiled, "I'm surprised you remembered. It's this weekend. I'm ready. We've got about two hundred pumpkins picked and ready to load up for the pumpkin patch at the festival. Hawthorne will help me, and I've got another friend coming as well."

"How is Hawthorne? It's been ages since I heard from him," Harrison mused.

"He's really good right now, actually. He's almost dating Avery Chase, do you remember her at all?" Harrison shook his head, and Poppy shrugged, "Well, she moved back from Colorado and they hit it off after all these years."

"How do you almost date someone?" he asked with a raised eyebrow.

Poppy laughed and explained Hawthorne's obvious crush on her childhood friend.

"I hope it works out for him. Do you think you could ever fall for someone you knew so long ago?" he asked, and Poppy glanced up sharply from her bread, her eyes meeting his. His question sounded casual and Poppy kicked herself for reading into it. Harrison didn't even know what he was asking. Looking into his eyes across the candlelit table, Poppy was terribly afraid the answer was yes.

She compressed the fluffy bread into a tight ball under the table. "I'm not sure. On the one hand, it's nice to have history with someone. Like Avery and Hawthorne weren't really even friends, but they knew each other. But sometimes, history isn't always good," she swallowed the lump in her throat, "and it can be hard to move past."

Harrison leaned across the table toward her, reaching his hand across the white tablecloth. "Poppy, the reason I wanted to—"

"Here we are," the waitress's cheery voice interrupted him. "Eggplant Parmesan for you," she laid the steaming plates in front of them, forcing Harrison to lean back, "and Chicken Marsala for the senator."

Harrison gave the waitress his politician smile, but Poppy was grateful for the interruption. Had she revealed too much when answering his question? Did *he* think it was possible to fall for someone from your past?

Instead, she focused on the food in front of her, quietly requesting more bread because obviously, carbs make everything better. Harrison glanced up at her, just as she put a piece of eggplant into her mouth. "Would you mind if I prayed?"

Poppy nearly choked and her mind rapidly considered her options. She could discretely spit out the bite. Yuck. Or she could finish chewing, forcing Harrison to awkwardly wait for her before praying.

She covered her mouth with her hand and tried to chew quickly. Ouch, it was super-hot. She nodded at Harrison to go ahead and pray, but he just smiled warmly and chuckled. No politician smile for her, this was the real deal.

Finally, the bite was done, "That would be nice, thank you."

Harrison held out his hand across the table and Poppy laid her hand in it. Harrison prayed, but Poppy didn't register a single word of it, too distracted by the warm, strong hands of Harrison Coulter. What was it about praying with someone and holding their hand that was so intimate? She was pretty sure it wasn't just the physical contact. She knew Harrison had solid faith when they were friends, but she had never been sure if it had stayed strong during and after college. Despite all the politicians who claimed to be Christians, Poppy knew it was an easy claim to make and a much harder one to live out.

"Thank you, most of all, for bringing Poppy back into my life. Amen," he finished, gently squeezing her hand before releasing it. Poppy felt that squeeze as though it had been her heart he held.

"Okay, Harrison. You have got to tell me what is going on. Why the sudden interest in being friends again?"

Harrison looked up from his plate, his dark eyes on hers, and set down his silverware. "Okay, so you know I've been involved with the state government for about six years." Poppy nodded and he continued, "Well, I have been approached about running for governor during the next election cycle."

Poppy's eyes widened in surprise. "Wow, Harrison. That is huge. Is that what you want?"

Harrison smirked, "That's a good question. Some days I'm not even sure I want to be a senator, let alone take on something bigger. But when I first got into public service, it was because I really felt like God was calling me there. And the more I pray about this now, the more I feel the same way." Harrison's voice quieted as he got more excited, "Poppy, I could do so much good for people as the governor. I feel like God is calling me to be a leader that steps out in faith and leads by example."

Poppy swelled with pride for her old friend. "That's wonderful. What do you need from me? I'm sure the IOSFA and the Southwest Indiana Farmers would endorse you, but I'm hardly the person to talk to about that..." She was still confused.

Harrison shook his head and sighed, "This is harder than I expected." He rubbed a hand over his jaw and straightened his tie. "Poppy, I know this is going to sound a little crazy. But I'd like you to marry me."

She froze, a bite of eggplant halfway to her mouth. What had he just said? She blinked slowly and set down her fork. He wanted to marry her? Nope. Not possible. A joke? That was the only logical explanation. She started to laugh, her loud guffaws making Harrison look around. "Oh my word, you really had me going there. Marry you!" Harrison's eyes grew wide, and he shushed her.

"Poppy," he whispered, waiting for her laughter to subside. "I'm not joking."

Her mouth hung open and she threw her hands in the air. "Are you crazy, Harrison? You must have lost your ever-loving mind!" Poppy shut her eyes and rubbed her temples. This was not happening.

"We were really good friends once, weren't we?"

Poppy's eyes flew open and she glared at him, "That was more than ten years ago, Harrison. We barely know each other! I can't—" She glanced around, suddenly conscious of her volume as she finished with a whisper, "I can't marry you!"

"Just hear me out. You aren't seeing anyone."

"I could be! You don't know me, Harrison." Poppy's anger was rising. How dare he assume she would fall at his feet and accept this... proposal.

Harrison hung his head, "You're right. I should have asked. But you didn't say anything about a boyfriend at the Gala. You can tell me now."

Poppy crossed her arms. "I'm not seeing anyone," she admitted reluctantly.

One of his non-campaign smiles emerged, and Poppy stared at the bread on her plate. Somehow, Harrison had managed to ruin homemade bread. "Neither am I. Plus, we are compatible." She scoffed and he repeated himself, "We *are* compatible. We share the same faith, the same background. I think we could be happy together."

"Why on earth would you want to get married?" Maybe she needed to suggest he see a psychologist. Psychiatrist? Whichever one it was, Harrison needed a professional.

"I don't, really," he admitted, "but the odds of me getting elected Governor as a 32-year-old bachelor are nonexistent. At least if I am married, I've got a real shot. Neil thinks if I marry—"

"I'm sorry, Neil thinks?" Poppy questioned sharply.

"My political advisor. He thinks that if I marry

someone who shares my love for Indiana, we can win."

Poppy was speechless. She had literally dreamed about this moment and filled notebooks with her name doodled as Mrs. Poppy Coulter. This was some sort of cruel twist of fate. I wish to marry Harrison Coulter. Wish granted—but he doesn't love you. He only wants you because you'll make a good trophy wife.

"Poppy, please, at least think about it. We could do so many things together, and I already know I won't ask anyone else. It's you or no one."

That didn't even make sense. If he was just looking for someone to help him get elected, why did it matter if it was her? There were probably hundreds of women who would jump at the chance to marry Harrison Coulter. After all, he was handsome, successful, and—it would seem—still a pretty good guy.

"Harrison, this is crazy. Why would I marry you? I barely even know you." Harrison hung his head.

"Honestly, I don't know. I've just been praying you'd say yes. I'm hoping you might see the same potential I do. Don't you see what we could do?"

But Poppy could only think of what they *couldn't* do. Would marrying Harrison be a forever commitment? Marriage was supposed to be for life—'til death do us part! Even if it wasn't for love, she would never agree to a marriage with a built-in escape plan. Would it mean giving up her dream of having kids? Poppy wasn't ready to give up on the idea of finding true love and a happily ever after! She might be twenty-nine years old, but that hardly made her an old maid who should jump at anything less than true love.

She shifted in her chair, wishing she could get up and pace. "Harrison, have you even thought about this?"

"I promise, Poppy, I've thought of literally nothing but this for a month."

Even with a month, Poppy wasn't sure she would be able to process this bombshell. "What does it even look like? You and I both know what the Bible says about marriage. It's forever. It's not like this is some movie where we get married to get you citizenship and then get a divorce later."

"I agree. This would be a lifetime commitment." He spoke so matter-of-factly, calm and collected, all Poppy wanted to do was throw water on him and prove he was some sort of robot-alien imposter.

"Are you serious? You barely know me, Harrison!

And you think you are ready to commit to forever with me?"

Harrison smiled at her and reached across the table to take her hand. His skin was warm against hers, and the contact stopped her fidgeting at the first touch. "Poppy, it may have been ten years, but I still know you. I know you are kind and generous. I know you love the land and stewarding it to the best of your ability. I know you love your family more than I could ever imagine. I know you would be loyal and honest, and you would keep me grounded if I were to be given the opportunity to lead our state." His gentle words eased her racing pulse and settled her objections. "That's more than enough for me, Poppy."

"I just... This is crazy."

"I know. It definitely feels that way at first. But maybe the more you think about it, the more it will make sense. Maybe you could pray about it?" He asked with raised eyebrows, imploring her to reconsider her strong objections. "Poppy, if you say no, I'll hold off. But I know there is no marriage of true love in my future. And all things considered, a marriage to someone I used to consider my best friend? Sounds pretty good."

Poppy pulled her hand out of his, unable to think

with his skin against hers. She pressed her eyes against the headache forming there. Harrison could say all the right things, that was his job. But Poppy had to keep a clear head. This would change absolutely everything. And she couldn't make any decisions without thinking it through.

"Won't you stay for dessert? I thought we could share tiramisu to celebrate your birthday."

Poppy's mouth fell open. Tomorrow, she would turn thirty. Her family would decorate her bedroom and share an ice cream cake, like usual. Nothing special. Harrison remembering her birthday, though? That made her feel special, but she didn't want to examine exactly why. If his thoughtfulness didn't mean anything, maybe his inevitable thoughtlessness wouldn't hurt either. Considering how to respond, she twisted her ring, an opal birthstone she'd received from her godmother when she turned sixteen.

Shaking her head, she told him she needed to leave, but he made her promise to call him.

As she started to step away from the table, he said her name, the tenderness in his voice stopping her in her tracks. "Poppy? I want you to know, if there is anything I can do that would make this worth it to you—just say the word. I'll do it."

Poppy pressed her lips together and nodded curtly, desperate to make her escape from the restaurant and his presence. Somehow, she knew things would never be the same. Whether she said yes or refused, her entire life would be polarized by this event. Harrison Coulter had asked her to marry him. What on earth was she going to do about it?

7

Harrison left the restaurant unsure of where things stood. All things considered, it had gone better than it could have. Part of him had expected a slap in the face, even if it wasn't Poppy's style. He'd actually had time to make most of his arguments.

Now, all he could do was pray and wait. He spent most of his time in Terre Haute until January, with a few exceptions for holiday parties in Indianapolis. But he had work to catch up on at the office. His work at the law firm was often pushed to the back burner while he was on senate business. Luckily, he was one of several partners in the firm, and he had a limited number of clients and hours to account for.

It was almost Thanksgiving, so it would be nice to be around home for a few days. He needed to see his parents. Plus, while he was here, maybe he could spend some more time with Poppy and make her realize that marrying him wouldn't be such a terrible idea.

With that in mind, Harrison went to the Harvest festival in Minden on Saturday. Minden was a bit of a drive from Terre Haute, but not far from his parents' house where he grew up. Harrison walked through the Harvest Festival, flooded with memories of the community tradition. The familiar hay bale maze, food trucks and carnival game booths took him back in time.

Today, live music from the small stage filled the air and he was drawn toward the perennial favorite, the Bloom's Farm Pumpkin Patch, where Poppy was currently manning a cheerfully decorated table overlooking her corner of the park. He hadn't heard from her since their dinner, and it felt a bit like ambushing her. He couldn't help but smile as Poppy chatted with a small child, her face full of excitement as the little girl proudly showed off the pumpkin she had chosen from the display laid out in the grass.

One of Poppy's sisters was there with her, and Poppy leaned over to whisper something to her. He watched for a moment, a bit shell-shocked. If his crazy plan worked, he could be married to this lovely woman. Poppy radiated something beautiful from deep within her. She had always been a wellspring of joy and goodness. What had happened all those years ago to make them fall away? Their friendship had been perfect. No pressure, no games. Others had always acted like it was impossible neither ever had feelings, but they were wrong. He and Poppy had been close, and both of them understood that it was just friendship. It hadn't been strong enough to survive the distance though, which was admittedly his fault. Harrison hadn't been willing to put in the effort of a long-distance friendship at the time. Would their newly rekindled connection be strong enough to survive marriage? Even if it were a marriage of convenience?

Harrison walked up to the booth and Poppy's eyes widened when she looked up at him from her chair.

"Harrison? Why—what are you doing here?"

"Just enjoying an old, local tradition. Figured while I was in the area visiting my parents tonight, I might as well drop by." He glanced at Poppy's sister, noticing the expensive camera around her neck. "Hi,

I'm Harrison Coulter. I'm afraid I can't quite remember your name."

The woman cleared her throat quietly, "I'm Lavender."

He flashed a smile, "Nice to meet you, Lavender. Mind if I borrow your sister for a bit?"

Lavender's mouth fell open, and she nodded with wide eyes.

Poppy gestured to the children crawling around the pumpkin patch, "I really shouldn't—"

He ignored her objections and spoke to Lavender, "Thanks. I'll have her back in thirty minutes."

Lavender glanced at Poppy and then back at him with a sly smile. "Take all the time you need. I've got things handled here."

With that settled, he took Poppy's hand, thrilled when she didn't pull away. He held her hand as they walked around the festival. "You know she is going to tell my entire family about this little exchange, right?" Poppy said once they were out of earshot.

"Doesn't bother me at all," he replied. "In fact, I was thinking when we've got this all worked out, it would be good to spend some time with you on the farm and get reacquainted."

"Harrison, I still don't know about all this. I've been praying and thinking about it, but I'm just..."

She stopped and pulled them off the sidewalk so they were out of the way. "I can't get over the crazy factor. And I don't know if I am ready to give up on marrying someone I love. I still want my happily ever after."

Harrison frowned. He hadn't considered that. He was asking Poppy to forego ever finding her Prince Charming. His heart sank as he realized she still wanted a fairy tale ending. Could he give her that? Their happily ever after would be different, but that didn't mean it wouldn't be full of blessings. He swallowed nervously and asked gently, "Don't you think we could be happy?"

Poppy looked up at him, and she sighed. "I don't know Harrison. I'd like to think so, but I'm not sure. Farming is my life! Can I really be the first lady of Indiana? And what happens if you lose the campaign or leave politics? And we are still married for the rest of our lives?"

Harrison ran a hand over his jaw. "I don't know, Poppy. All I know is that God is asking me to run for governor. And that you are the only person I want by my side when I do it."

Poppy ground her toe into the frozen dirt of Minden Park, staring straight ahead at the glossy buttons of Harrison's black winter coat. She desperately wanted to say yes, to agree to marry Harrison and start building a life with him. She was pathetic! How could she even think of tying her life to someone who didn't love her, who had hurt her so badly all those years ago?

Poppy had spent less than seven hours with the man in the last five years. How could he be so convinced they were compatible? Still, all the arguments he had made at the restaurant had rattled around her head for days. They could make a difference. Friendship was a good foundation for marriage. Then there was his last statement. If there was anything he could do to make her agree to it, he would do it.

The more she'd been reading up on The Farm Business Act, the more worried she was. They weren't simply making it more expensive to run a small farm by stripping away tax incentives, they were actively promoting selling to larger corporations. It would kill the business of local family operations. Would marrying Harrison give her a way to save her farm?

"What do you know about the bill Senator Hawkins is proposing? The Farm Business Act."

Harrison frowned, "Not exactly what I came to talk about, but I think I've heard a bit about it. He is touting it as a big economic development and job creation measure."

Poppy scoffed, "I'm sure he is. What it's going to do is make it way harder to survive as a small farm. Right now, we rely on the farm-friendly tax laws that lower the tax liability for holdings under 400 acres." Andrew and Lisha would be hit too, not to mention hundreds of other farmers around the state. The only people who would benefit? The owners, typically corporations, of operations larger than 1000 acres. "Harrison, tell me you don't support that bill." She pleaded.

Harrison frowned, "I hadn't actually thought too much about it. But if it is framed how you say it is, I would probably vote against it."

Poppy's shoulders sagged in relief. "Okay, good." That was easier than she expected. But that was one vote. A single stake in the fight for small farms, when she knew it would be an ongoing battle. If she were married to the governor, or even to a senator, he could make a real difference.

Harrison continued, "Of course. It would look

strange for me to vote for a bill that would jeopardize my wife's pride and joy." His eyes danced with laughter, and Poppy smiled. Leave it to Harrison to act like she had already agreed to his crazy proposal. It was confident and presumptuous, but it made her laugh. He had always made her laugh.

Maybe they could make this work, for the good of the farm. And yes, maybe just a little for the lovesick teenager who always wanted to be Harrison's right-hand woman. But this time, she would make sure she protected her heart. Poppy looked past him, toward the stage where a goofy musician was entertaining children, "Okay, then. If you will commit to *a lifetime* of using your office to support small farms, I will stand by your side," she swallowed and looked up to meet his gaze, "as your wife."

Harrison grinned and wrapped her in a hug. "Thank you, Poppy. You won't regret it."

She snuggled into the warmth of his body, a welcome reprieve from the chilly air, and inhaled the spicy scent of his cologne. Closing her eyes to the unexpected sting of tears, she prayed he was right.

8

Harrison held Poppy's hand as they continued walking. At this point, it didn't matter who saw, it would only strengthen their story. Plus, he kind of liked the feel of her hand in his. Harrison had already talked to Neil about the best strategy, and getting married as soon as possible was important. He would need to announce his candidacy next fall at the latest, but having the marriage be established before then would help squash any speculation that it was only a political stunt.

It would be strange, to be affectionate and physical with Poppy, despite the terms of their agreement. Would they share a room? His blood heated at the thought. As they turned a corner in the hay bale maze, Harrison cleared his throat. "Should we talk about what this looks like?"

Poppy tucked a strand of hair behind her ear and shrugged while avoiding his gaze, "I guess we should. Do I still get to be in charge of Bloom's Farm? I can't imagine leaving." Poppy bit her lip, and the worry in her eyes made him stop their leisurely stroll.

Harrison placed his hands on her shoulders. "You can stay on Bloom's Farm as long as you want to. You'll have to come with me to the capital pretty often, but I think we can make it work. Until I'm elected governor, I technically have to reside in Terre Haute, since that is my district. But after that, we can live wherever you'd like."

Poppy's eyes widened, "Oh, I guess we will live together, right?"

Harrison smiled, "Well, yes. Ideally I would live with my wife—at least some of the time."

Poppy blushed. "Will, um... will we, you know... *be married*? In the full sense of the word?" She pinched her eyes closed, mortified by her own question. Harrison's smiled broadened. She was adorable when she was embarrassed.

He reached out to stroke her cheek, the most endearing shade of red. He considered his words and spoke quietly. "I don't know, Poppy. I think we'll take it one day at a time as far as that goes. But I suspect forever is a really long time." What would they look like in twenty years? Fifty? "And I think God is faithful and good." Forever together didn't necessarily mean love, but Harrison did believe what he said. God was good.

Poppy tipped her head to lean into his caress, and he pulled her close. She spoke, the sound muffled by his coat. "My mom always says that love is a choice."

Harrison considered her words. Was love a choice? Or a feeling? He took a step back, trying to create some distance between them. He wasn't ready for either one where Poppy was concerned. If she got too close, she would never stick around. And he needed to focus on getting elected. "I'm grateful you are doing this, Poppy. Right now, I think we simply view it as two friends making a commitment to pursue something together. Anything else is getting ahead of ourselves. Okay?"

Poppy's smile dimmed, and she nodded, turning away to continue down the empty hay bale aisle.

Harrison caught up with her in two strides. Had he said something wrong? Appearances mattered, but he cared about Poppy, too. "I know this is strange. And even though we will let our private life be whatever comes naturally, it's important we act like a married couple in public. Holding hands, hugs," he swallowed and forced himself to finish, "even brief kisses. No one can suspect this was anything but a romantic relationship that moved quickly to marriage."

Poppy was silent, but nodded her agreement. What was she thinking? Did she want to change her mind?

They continued walking, and hesitantly, Harrison reached his hand toward hers, brushing her fingertips. She turned her hand and curled her fingers around his, and every muscle relaxed in relief. It was something. He needed this to work. If Neil was right, which he usually was, Poppy was the key to the governor's mansion.

For a while, he let the conversation drift away from the serious matter at hand, and they chatted about the farm. They bought hot chocolate from Chrissy and the B&J Bistro table and wandered around the festival. It felt like almost like a date. A date with his *fiancée*. At the word, his mind took off on an endless list of things he needed to do. She needed a ring. They needed to set up a ceremony. Would Poppy want a big wedding? Or a small, intimate affair?

"Poppy, do you have any idea what kind of wedding you'd like?"

She replied with a noncommittal shrug and asked a question of her own. "When do we need to have the ceremony?"

Ideally, they would be married for a year before the campaign was announced next September. But they were already too late for that. "The sooner the better, so it doesn't seem linked to the campaign announcement next fall. But we can wait a little bit, if you need us to."

Harrison held his breath, waiting for her response. Even though she'd agreed, he was walking on eggshells, afraid she would change her mind any moment. Poppy stared over his shoulder for several moments, her voice calm and emotionless as she answered. "I'll tell my family we are dating at Thanksgiving, and then maybe we can get married right before Christmas."

"That sounds great." Harrison would agree to just about anything at this point.

"I'm still pretty sure they will have a few things to say about such a quick wedding," she said, meeting his gaze again.

He definitely would if Easton got married that quickly. "Probably. Do you want to tell them about the arrangement?" The more people they told, the trickier it would be. But if Poppy needed to tell them, then they could make it work.

She shook her head. "I don't want them to suspect that it is anything less than real for us. My family will for sure try to talk me out of it. But if I can convince them that is real, I'll be way better off."

Knowing his time was almost up, he led them back to the pumpkin patch table, giving Lavender a warm smile. "I'll call you, okay?" Poppy nodded and he leaned down to whisper in her ear, "I'll be in touch. We can start on the arrangements for you to officially become Mrs. Harrison Coulter."

Harrison left Poppy there to answer the inevitable questions of her younger sister and made his way back to his car. He headed out of Minden, with a quick survey of the town and the quaint Main Street shops, pleased to see new names and very few empty storefronts.

Fifteen minutes later, he pulled up to the gated entrance on the gravel road. Who really needed a gated front drive out here in the middle of nowhere? Still, it had been that way as long as he could remember. Neil might have played up his humble 'good ole boy' image during campaign stops, but the truth was, Harrison's family had money. Lots of money from lots of cattle owned by his grandfather, the former governor, and now his father.

He pulled into the circular drive and parked next to manicured evergreen bushes. There would be no gaudy Christmas lights from his mother. Marilyn Coulter would fit in better in Indianapolis or Chicago, but her devotion to his father meant she stayed and embraced rural Indiana. Perhaps it was better. Here, the Coulters were big fish in a small pond, and his mother could flaunt her status and her sons' achievements. Well, one of her sons anyway. Harrison's brother, Easton, hadn't exactly lived up to the Coulter family expectations.

Harrison knocked on the door before opening it and yelling into the large foyer. "Hello? Mom, Dad!"

He stepped out of his shoes, knowing that if he tracked dirt into his mother's house she was likely to make him sweep it up, despite his status as a state senator. Movement at the top of the staircase caught his eye and he watched as his mother floated down the steps. "Harrison! I'm so glad you are here. Reggie, Harrison is here!" she yelled toward the back of the house before wrapping him in her arms. His mom was at least affectionate with her children, he suspected to make up for the cool disapproval from their father.

"Hey, Mom."

"How long will you be here? Your room is ready upstairs," she said excitedly.

Harrison winced, "Sorry, Mom. I've got to go back to Terre Haute tonight, but I'll be back next week for Thanksgiving."

His mom's shoulders sagged in disappointment, then straightened, "Have you heard from Easton? I keep hoping he'll come home to see us for the holidays." Easton was famous for ignoring their parents' phone calls, but he usually answered Harrison, or at least texted back from whatever Caribbean island he was currently sailing around.

"Sorry, I haven't." At the sadness in his mother's eyes, he ducked to meet her gaze, "I'll try to call him tonight, okay?"

"Thanks, sweetie. I just worry about him so much. All those tropical storms and he barely even lets us know he is still alive!"

"I know, Mom. I'll call, okay?" His brother had ditched the corporate world and now spent his days taking tourists on chartered excursions on his sailboat. It wouldn't be hard to imagine his little beach house battered by a hurricane, or worse, Easton stuck at sea during a squall. Still, Easton was a grown man, despite his tendency to act like a teenager, and the best things Harrison could do was encourage their relationship and pray.

Reginald Coulter came around the corner, his suspenders over a long-sleeved canvas work shirt. His father certainly didn't look like the millionaire he was. "Harrison, you look well." His father's detached tone was unsurprising.

"Hey, Dad," he responded and accepted his father's hand. "How's it going around here?" he asked.

His mother brushed past him and waved him in. "Come on back to the kitchen so we can chat. I'll have Tina make you a cup of coffee."

They walked through the living room and into the large, open kitchen and dining room. Soaring windows overlooked the pasture behind the house where cows dotted the landscape.

His dad rambled about the farm, complaining about the price of beef—too low, and the price of corn—too high. "How are you, Harrison? Still playing politician instead of focusing on your law office?"

Harrison glanced at his mom, who smiled apologetically. Reginald Coulter had none of the political ambitions of Harrison's grandpa and firmly believed money was the best way to make a difference in the world. "I have two more years on this term, but you already know that."

When Harrison had become a lawyer, his dad had been disappointed he didn't want to run the ranch. When he became a politician, he moaned about how Harrison was wasting his potential. When Harrison had passed his first piece of legislation, Reginald-the-Great lectured him about how it should have done more. That had been painful.

Harrison was proud of the work he did as a senator. This year, he was introducing a huge piece of education legislation. The Teaching Excellence and Curriculum Harmony (TEACH) Act was desperately needed and would improve education initiatives throughout the state. But if it didn't come with zeroes on the end, Reginald Coulter didn't care. No matter what he did, Harrison was starting to realize it would never be quite enough for his father. It was better he held himself at a distance, even with his own parents. That didn't seem healthy, but with his dad's opinionated nature, it was better not to open up too much.

Kind of like with Stacy. The more she knew, the more it hurt.

"I don't know how or why you do it. Splitting your time between home and Indianapolis. How many miles did you put on that little car this year? Wouldn't worry about it so much if you had bought American, like a true patriot."

Harrison fought the eye-roll and responded to the first comment, "Too many. But I don't mind the drive."

His mother chimed in, "Well, I'm sure it makes it hard to have a relationship. At least you don't have a family you are leaving behind every time you have to travel."

Harrison cleared his throat and laughed. It sounded weak and forced, even to him. He needed to tell his parents. "Actually, that's one thing I wanted to talk to you about."

"Oh," his mother exclaimed, "are you finally seeing someone? What is her name? Do we know her? Is she coming for Thanksgiving? I need to redecorate the guest room!"

"Calm down, Marilyn. Let the boy speak," his father said.

"Relax, Mom. I'm not springing anyone on you for Thanksgiving." His mother frowned, probably disappointed that she wouldn't get to redecorate. "Actually, I wanted to tell you that I'm getting married."

His dad choked on his coffee and coughed. His

mother squealed and Harrison winced at the high-pitched noise.

"Were you even dating anyone, Harrison?"

"How could you not tell me that you were serious with someone? Is she from Indianapolis? It's not Stacy, is it?" his mother badgered.

Harrison chuckled, "No, it's not Stacy. Actually, it's Poppy Bloom."

His father frowned, "One of Keith and Laura's girls? With the ridiculous flower names?" Harrison nodded, though annoyance surged at his father's description.

His mother looked confused. "But I haven't even heard you mention her since high school. Where did this come from?"

Harrison started to explain, "Well, it's a bit complicated. You guys know I've been considering running for governor, right?" his mother nodded proudly and his father rolled his eyes. "Well, it would be nearly impossible for me to get elected while I'm still single." Understanding lit his mother's face and she covered her gasp, he continued before she could interrupt. "And since I have no plans to ever fall in love or marry otherwise, I needed to find a wife who would take this journey with me."

"Oh, Harrison. This is crazy. You can't ask this

girl to marry you if you don't love her!" his mother admonished. "And why would you say you'll never fall in love?"

"I already asked her," he said while his mother clucked her tongue, "and she said yes."

"Why on earth would she say yes? Is she in trouble?" Harrison's father stood and began to pace. "Pregnant? Or, more likely, she's just after your money. Harrison, this is ridiculous."

Harrison jerked away from the accusations. "What? No, nothing like that. Poppy would never do that. She just wants to make a difference with me. She cares about her farm and her family more than anything, and she wants to make sure the government continues to value those things as well."

"I don't know, son. This seems like a bad idea," his mother looked at him with a wrinkle of concern.

Harrison stood, "I know it seems crazy. But for the last month I have done nothing but pray about whether or not I should pursue the office of governor." His dad scoffed at the mention of Harrison's faith, "And since Neil told me I should think about a wife, the only person I could think about marrying is Poppy. I have to believe God is orchestrating this."

Throwing his hands in the air, Reginald responded, "Harrison, you aren't thinking clearly.

What if the press finds out? Our family would never live down the shame."

"They won't. Poppy and I are friends. There is no reason people wouldn't believe we fell in love and got married."

"This seems so dishonest, sweetie. Are you sure this is what God would have you do? What happens if you fall in love with someone else? Or if Poppy does?"

Harrison frowned at the thought of Poppy leaving him for someone else. "Mom, we have both agreed that this is a forever commitment. In our eyes, this is a very real marriage. Perhaps with a foundation that is a little unconventional in this country, but very much the real deal." He shrugged, "People have arranged marriages all the time."

"In countries halfway around the world, son! Not in the Midwest!" his dad's outburst brought wide-eyed looks from everyone, including Tina who had been quietly preparing coffee in the adjacent kitchen. Harrison tried to defuse the conversation.

"I know it seems crazy, but trust me. Please? Marrying Poppy is my path to the governor's office. And from there, I can make such an incredible impact."

"Bah, you are just like your grandfather."

Harrison tried not to smile as his dad marched out of the kitchen. There were worse people to be compared to.

"It's the impact it might have on you that I'm worried about," his mother said with tears in her eyes. She patted his cheek and then swept out of the kitchen. This conversation was over, at least for now. Harrison had a feeling next week would be more of the same. But by that time, he would have a ring in his pocket. Maybe he could convince Poppy to come over. If his parents could just see what he saw when he looked at her, maybe they would agree she was the perfect person to stand with him as he followed God's plan.

9

As promised, Harrison called his brother, Easton, that evening. If anyone understood what it was like to deal with his parents, it was Easton. Harrison settled onto his sofa, his cat quickly jumping up to join him.

"It's eighty degrees and sunny here, man," his brother said by way of greeting. "What's it like there? Wait, wait, don't tell me. Forty and drizzling rain?"

Harrison smiled. "Not quite that bad, but there is snow in the forecast next week. You going to come home and see it?"

"Sorry. I think I'm going to have to take a hard pass on that one." No surprise there. As strained as Harrison's relationship was with his parents, Easton's was a hundred times worse.

"Come on, Easton. You haven't come home in a year. Mom and Dad are worried about you."

"Mom might be. But you and I both know the only thing Dad is worried about is whether I've already blown my trust fund and whether formally disowning a son would be bad for business."

Harrison laughed and threw an arm over the back of the couch. "Well, it is called Coulter and Sons Ranch."

"Exactly. And yet neither of us are involved. It must keep him up at night." Easton didn't sound too concerned.

Fiona started purring and he scratched her ears. "Maybe he is still hoping?"

"Hoping for another son, perhaps."

"Yes, what a disappointment we must be. You abandoning your successful career as an engineer so you could sail the seven seas. And me with the audacity to become a politician."

Easton scoffed, "Come on, Harrison. You think Sir Reginald the Uptight places us at the same level? You might be in politics, but at least that comes with something Dad understands. Power. Me? I've got a boat I can sleep in and the same four pairs of shorts I rotate through. If we are playing the 'who is a bigger disappointment' game, I think I've got you beat."

Harrison smiled. "Maybe so."

"I know you think you were doing your own thing and stepping out against the expectations of our parents, but Harrison—you played right into them. You care too much to let them down. Mom couldn't be prouder of her son, the senator. And Dad? He'd never admit it, but we both know he just wishes you wanted to take over the ranch. Other than that? You are a Coulter, through and through."

He dropped his head on the back of the couch and rolled his eyes. His older brother was just full of wisdom tonight. Such insight from a thousand miles away. "Today he said I was just like Grandpa and stormed out of the room."

"See?"

Changing the subject, Harrison circled back. "I miss you, Easton. It would be good to see you. Maybe you could come back up for Christmas, at least?"

"I'll think about it." That was as close to a commitment as he was going to get, so Harrison let it go. "Look, man, I've got a sunset sail scheduled with some honeymooners. I'll let you know about Christmas."

"Be safe," Harrison said, but the line had already disconnected.

10

On Thanksgiving morning, Poppy was in the kitchen with Daisy, Lavender, Lily and their mother. Avery and Hawthorne were going for a morning horseback ride before everyone came back to the house for dinner.

Poppy feigned interest in the Macy's Thanksgiving Day parade and ran through her big announcement in her head. Today, she was going to tell her family she was dating Harrison Coulter. Her mother would be happy for her. Daisy would be the least surprised, since she'd caught her on the phone with him. Lily would probably shake her head in disappointment. When she'd been distraught about Harrison's lack of interest and insensitive actions, Poppy had confided in her oldest sister. Lily, a self-proclaimed skeptic of love, had advised Poppy to move on and never look back. Which Poppy had done, until a month ago.

She would lay the groundwork today, by telling her family she was dating Harrison. Then, she could invite them to the wedding right before Christmas. It would be fast, but the plans would be in the open.

As the giant Snoopy float came on-screen, the front door crashed open and Avery Chase came running in, calling for Daisy. Between gasps of air, she explained, "Your dad had a stroke. Down at the animal barn. The ambulance is on the way."

"Is he okay?" Getting no answer, she quickly stepped to Daisy's side as she rushed to the door. Her mom was already gone, moving faster than all of them.

At Lavender's suggestion, Poppy adjusted her course to head for the garage and her mom's SUV. With shaking fingers, Poppy grabbed the key from a hook by the door and punched the garage door button on the wall.

She whispered desperate prayers as she turned on the car and pulled onto the gravel drive heading toward the barn. She spotted her mother jogging on the road, her long lilac cardigan trailing in the cold wind.

After their mother climbed in, Poppy drove the five of them to the barn. Where was Avery? Her mother stepped out as Poppy parked the SUV and ran inside the barn, calling her husband's name.

Poppy and her sisters followed, and as Poppy's eyes adjusted to the light inside the stables, she saw Hawthorne cradling their father's limp body. Her mother kneeled on the floor beside them, her husband's face in her hands as she moaned.

Unable to watch, Poppy walked back outside to flag down the emergency workers. She hopped on an ATV and whipped it onto the gravel, heading for the front gate. She parked below the rustic sign announcing the entrance of Bloom's Farm and Vineyard that Hawthorne had made last year.

The icy wind tore across the open pastures, cutting through Poppy's floral cotton blouse and swirling around the gypsy-style skirt she wore. Her face was numb, and it wasn't until she tasted salt that Poppy realized she was crying.

Finally, the sound of a siren reached her ears, carried by the wind, and she perked up, straining for a glimpse of the ambulance. When she saw them, Poppy stood and waved her arms to get their attention. She turned the ATV around and led them past the bed-and-breakfast to the barn.

Poppy sank into bed that night more exhausted than she had ever been, even after full days of digging potatoes or hauling watermelons. Emotional exhaustion was somehow more draining than physical labor, and today had been the worst day she could remember.

Her father was unconscious in a hospital bed, the effects of the stroke still undetermined. Right now, she couldn't think about anything except whether her father would be okay. Keith Bloom *was* Bloom's Farm. The idea of him being gone was unfathomable.

Hawthorne was missing. Poppy had called Avery, but no one had seen her brother since early this afternoon. All her plans to tell her family about Harrison were on hold. Harrison had texted his usual goodnight message, with a bit of added commentary about Thanksgiving with his parents.

Thanksgiving was strained. But Mom wants to meet you. She asked why you didn't come.

I'm sure they will love you.

Poppy couldn't bring herself to reply, but Harrison deserved to know why she was going to have to pull back. Having two families was twice as complicated, and twice as tiresome. She only had enough energy for her own family, let alone enough to deal with Harrison's.

Text messages from her siblings came in rapidly, arranging for a family meeting in the morning. Apparently Hawthorne had been found. With a prayer of thanks, she replied to the group text.

I'll make breakfast for everyone.

Everything would be easier to tackle with a full stomach.

She opened her conversation with Harrison again, skimming the chain of messages she hadn't answered all day.

No worries. Bigger issue here. Dad had a stroke.

Moments after she hit send, Harrison's name appeared with an incoming call. She ignored it and tapped another text.

Too tired, going to bed.

His reply came quickly and Poppy struggled to keep her eyes focused.

Praying. Talk tomorrow?

Quickly, she thumbed the heart picture and fell asleep with her phone in her hand, too tired to second-guess her choice.

~

Four days later, Harrison was back at work and frustrated. When they talked on Friday, Poppy had been distracted and upset, which he knew was understandable. Obviously, her world had just been turned upside down a bit. But he wanted her to turn to him when things were in turmoil, not shut him out.

What was he supposed to do to help if she would barely talk to him? Her family still, presumably, had no idea they were involved. He was tempted to just show up at the farm. Actually, that wasn't such a bad idea. Leaving his office early, he ignored the wide-eyed looks from Janet, his paralegal. Harrison ran back to his house and grabbed some jeans and an old sweatshirt from college.

If Poppy wouldn't talk to him, he would go to her, and she could put him to work. It was the only way he could think to help, other than what he'd already done by calling and directing all the medical bills for Keith Bloom to be billed directly to him. That didn't seem like nearly enough, but Harrison had more money than he knew what to do with. Helping his soon-to-be wife's family seemed like a good place to start.

When Harrison drove up to the farm, he became acutely aware of how much it had changed over the years. A large barn, with iron accents and a wood-shingled roof stood off to the right as he came in the main drive. The old, run-down house he vaguely remembered had been completely redone and a wooden sign in the front yard declared "Bloom's Farm Bed-and-Breakfast" in neat green letters.

He found a barn surrounded by fields of empty soil and parked in the gravel lot next to Poppy's familiar gray truck. At least he knew she was here.

Harrison wandered into the barn, looking for Poppy, but it was eerily still. He walked past stacks of seed bags and an old tractor sitting next to a shiny new one. At the other end of the building, there was an open interior door with light pouring into the dark hallway, and he headed toward it.

Inside, he found Poppy with her head buried in her hands. At his footsteps, she looked up and his heart cracked at the sight of his friend with tears in her eyes. She looked shocked at his presence and turned away, but he swept her into his arms and ran his hand over her braided hair and her upper back. He whispered, "It's okay, Poppy. It's going to be okay."

She wriggled, a half-hearted attempt to push him away, but he wasn't going anywhere. Poppy sobbed into his shoulder, the T-shirt growing damp beneath her cheek, and he felt his own sorrow at her obvious pain. She felt soft and warm in his arms, a perfect fit. Had they ever been this close before? Harrison wanted to make her smile and see the joy she always radiated. He even wanted her to give him a snarky comment and the sassy eyebrow raise he'd seen so many times.

Harrison had missed her. Perhaps without even realizing it, he'd needed his friend all these years. Was this his second chance?

Whatever happened, Harrison wanted to be there for Poppy. She had come through for him, agreeing to his crazy idea of getting married. He would be a shoulder to lean on when she was sad. It hardly seemed like enough. Still, as he sat there and stroked her hair, he wondered what exactly he had gotten himself into. This seemed like such a good idea only a few weeks ago, when the only thing on the line was an election. Now, he was afraid there was so much more at stake. Like, maybe, his heart.

11

The first few weeks of December passed in a blur, Poppy trying her best to manage her own job, pieces of her father's role, and help her mother cope with the sudden change. She went with her siblings to pick up Daisy's twin sister, Andi, and did her best to be her cheerful self. But the secret relationship with Harrison was still weighing her down. She hadn't gotten a chance to share at Thanksgiving. She didn't feel like she could tell her family now, though. The news seemed insignificant in the midst of the turmoil of dealing with her father's stroke.

Now, Daisy was having trouble with her bed-and-breakfast renovation, since the county inspector had apparently decided he had it out for the project.

It was rotten for Daisy, but it meant her nosiest sister was too preoccupied to notice when Poppy was tight-lipped.

Poppy considered telling her family nearly every time they were together, but it never seemed like the right time. Spending time together was out of the question with everything going on. Instead, she and Harrison texted and talked. She missed him, which seemed crazy, since they were just friends. She just had to keep reminding herself of that.

Can you still come to my holiday party for work tomorrow? I know things are still hard for you around home...

Poppy had agreed to go weeks ago, before everything happened. After all, that was kind of the whole point, right? To establish them as a couple? At least it was in Terre Haute, instead of all the way in Indianapolis like the IOSFA dinner.

She still wanted to go, eager to see Harrison again, despite her better judgment screaming that she was getting too attached. The only concern was that Poppy didn't want to get all dressed up at the farm and risk someone seeing her.

Could I get ready for the party at your house? I don't want anyone to ask why I'm all dressed up.

Sure. I'll leave your key under the mat.

He sent the address and the next afternoon, Poppy packed a duffel bag and stuffed it in the toolbox compartment in the bed of her truck.

When she opened the door to his house, it felt like breaking and entering. A gray tabby cat approached and made figure-eights between her legs, rubbing against her boots as though starved for attention. Poppy melted at the fact that Harrison had a cat. It was so unexpected and refreshing. He definitely struck her as more of a dog person. They had their share of barn cats around the farm but none so sweet as the soft cat currently purring under her caress. Quickly, she tapped out a message.

You own a cat?

I think, technically, Fiona owns me, right?

She smiled at his comment and set Fiona down before walking further into the house. Harrison's house was stylishly decorated and very clean. The couches looked impossibly comfortable and soft throw blankets were fanned in effortless perfection on the ottoman and across the back of an armchair. She fingered the soft cashmere of one of the blankets, a bright cheery yellow that carried through other accents in the room.

Poppy paused in the kitchen to get a glass of water, peeking in his fridge, surprised to see fresh produce in the crisper and more than takeout leftovers on the shelves. Perhaps she expected every bachelor to be like Hawthorne, who only ate vegetables if you included corn.

She wandered back through the space and found the bathroom down the hallway. The house was smaller than she'd imagined, knowing Harrison's upbringing. Had Marilyn seen this place?

Poppy set her duffel bag in the bathroom and shut the door, her mouth falling open when she found a garment bag hanging on the back of the door. Again? He had to be kidding. She sighed and unzipped the bag, curious what Harrison would have picked for her to wear tonight. The glittering emerald-green dress was incredible. Her own simple black cocktail dress hardly compared, but she wouldn't be wearing the dress Harrison picked.

She might be marrying him, but Poppy Bloom was *still* not an accessory he could control. He'd tried this before in Indianapolis and it hadn't worked. It wouldn't work this time, either. After her shower, Poppy wrapped her long hair up in a towel and slid her black dress over her head. With the glamorous dress sparkling in the mirror from behind, her own outfit looked depressing and drab. Would it be so bad to wear the dress he picked? She'd never been to a Christmas party for a law firm. Would she look out of place in her cheap, department store dress?

Poppy eyed the offending gown the entire time she put on her makeup and blow-dried her auburn hair into soft waves. The black dress she wore was fine. Totally fine. But... then again, she was going to marry Harrison, and this was a big deal for him. It was almost like a coming out party. Shouldn't she try to look her best? If not for Harrison, then for the public?

With a sigh, she peeled off the basic black sheath and held the hanger up to her body, letting the emerald gown drape over her.

She stepped into it, feeling incredibly sophisticated as the expensive dress floated down to her ankles and barely skimmed the floor. Poppy reached to grab the zipper near the small of her back and managed to pull it up only inches before it got stuck. "Shoot," she said, twisting and switching hands to try for better leverage.

"Everything okay in there?" Harrison called from outside the door with a quiet knock. Poppy froze like a deer in the headlights. He was home?

The stomping and bumping he'd heard stopped completely when he knocked on the door, and Harrison waited a beat before knocking again. "Poppy?"

"Umm, just a second," she called.

Harrison had come home fifteen minutes before and heard the sound of the blow dryer from the bathroom in the hallway. He'd been right to assume she would choose that one instead of the larger master bath. Poppy wasn't the type to snoop, but the thought of her in his bedroom and the bathroom he used every morning had him tugging on his collar.

He waited in the living room and checked his watch. They needed to be leaving soon but Poppy still wasn't out. What was taking so long?

Finally, the bathroom door opened and she stepped out, her hands behind her back and an embarrassed look on her face. He barely registered all of that beyond the fact that Poppy looked absolutely stunning. Her eyes were lined and shadowed, making the beautiful brown pop against her skin. Her lips glistened as though they'd just been thoroughly kissed and her earrings dangled, drawing his eyes to the slender line of her neck.

But then he saw the dress. His heart soared with victory when he realized she had actually agreed to wear the dress he had picked for her. Not only because it was obviously made for her, accentuating her natural curves, but because it was significant for her to choose the dress. As though she were choosing him at the same time.

"Harrison!" Her voice cut into his admiring and he jerked his gaze back up to her face. She watched him with amusement. "Yep, up here. Thanks. Can you help me with this?" She turned around so he could see the zipper, and his breath caught at the wide expanse of skin that greeted him when she turned. The back of the dress dipped low, leaving her upper back exposed, but the zipper was caught and his gaze dipped lower and lower and— "Are you going to help me or should I go put on my other dress?"

He stood and walked over to her, gently replacing her fingers on the zipper with his own. She pulled her hair to one side, revealing her shoulder blades and neck. He pulled it up gently, his fingers large and clumsy on the tiny clasp. Painstakingly slowly, the dress came together. Then he felt resistance and saw the zipper caught on the fabric. With a desperate prayer, he lowered the zipper an inch before gently tugging it back up. His knuckles grazed the warm skin of her back, and she shivered.

The zipper stopped, reaching the top of its climb, and Harrison held it, unwilling to let go. She was intoxicating. Quietly, he stepped close and skimmed his hand up her spine to her shoulder, leaning to the opposite side to lay a gentle kiss where the curve of her neck met her shoulder. He could see the tips of her lashes drift closed at the contact. Poppy didn't move a muscle as he whispered in her ear, "You will be the most beautiful woman in the room."

Then he forced himself to step back and take a deep breath. He had to fill his lungs with something other than the painfully tantalizing scent of her citrus shampoo.

Poppy dropped her hair, covering the expanse of skin he could swear sent sparks through his fingers and cleared her throat. "Are we ready to go?"

Harrison nodded and opened the door. Yep, they'd better get out of here before he decided maybe the Christmas party was less enticing than staying here alone with Poppy.

At the party, Harrison knew he could count on many of the partners drinking too much and sharing exaggerated stories from court cases won and lost. This year, it was hosted at the extravagant home of

Patrick Lauer, one of the oldest partners of the firm. Despite being held at a home instead of a fancy restaurant or hotel, Harrison knew from experience that he and Poppy would not be overdressed. Evening gowns sparkled under the lights, a bartender served drinks from a strategically placed station in the corner of the massive living room. Harrison's fingers rested gently on the small of Poppy's back, hoping to give her some reassurance. The comment he made earlier was accurate. His fiancée was the most beautiful woman in the room.

Poppy turned to him, "Do you know everyone here?" This was actually the more intimate party, but there were still more than forty people milling about. To get an invitation to this party, you had to be at least a partner. While only senior partners had equity in the firm, partners were granted voting rights and greater freedom to choose their clients. Harrison had been granted the privilege two years ago. While it had taken nearly everything he had to manage court cases and settlements alongside his senatorial duties, Harrison had been determined to be the best at both. The partners of the law firm apparently agreed and offered him a partnership.

"Patrick, I'd like you to meet my fiancée, Poppy.

Poppy, this is my boss, and our gracious host for the evening."

Mr. Lauer shook Poppy's hand and raised his eyebrows at Harrison. "I guess congratulations are in order, Senator?"

Harrison smiled and Patrick's wife, Denise, stepped up beside them. "Ah, Mrs. Lauer, you look beautiful this evening." He had never seen the elegant woman with a hair out of place, always perfectly serene. She was regal and beautiful, though with a fraction of the warmth that Poppy exuded. He had a little something planned to win her favor this evening though.

"Harrison, so nice to see you."

He gestured to Poppy, "My fiancée, Poppy Bloom."

Poppy smiled warmly. "Mrs. Lauer, I must say, your home is exquisite. Thank you for hosting this evening's festivities."

Harrison pulled the small box from his pocket and gave it to Denise."A little token of our appreciation for the host." Denise's face showed a note of surprise. "Please, go ahead and open it if you'd like."

Denise couldn't hide her pleasure when she saw the contents of the box. "Oh, Harrison, you charming devil. How did you know? Look, Patrick. Café Doka!"

Harrison's smile was genuine. "Patrick told me about your visit to Costa Rica and how much you loved their coffee. I ordered some directly from the plantation for you."

Denise glanced at Poppy, "You are a very lucky lady, Miss Bloom. I've been trying to set Harrison here up with our daughter for years, but he always put me off. Looking at the two of you, now I understand why."

Poppy blushed and felt Harrison's hand tighten on her waist. She looked up at him, her eyes landing on the strong cut of his jaw. "We're very excited," she said. When Harrison looked down at her, Poppy's heart started to race. There was something in his eyes she couldn't read. Approval? Or something more?

"Well, I'll let you two lovebirds enjoy the rest of the party. Thank you again for this, Harrison. It was very thoughtful of you."

"You'll get more each month—if I managed to place the order correctly," Harrison added with a self-deprecating grin.

Patrick slapped a hand on Harrison's shoulder, "I think you've made a friend for life, Harrison. There's no chance she'll let me fire you now!" His laughter boomed as he stepped away from them and joined another circle of guests.

Poppy smiled at the joke and turned to Harrison. "That *was* a very thoughtful gift."

Harrison stepped close, "What can I say? I'm a thoughtful guy." His flirtatious tone and confident wink had Poppy wobbling on her heels. If he turned his thoughtful charm towards her, Poppy was a goner.

The party was easy, surprisingly so for Poppy, who assumed she would be uncomfortable surrounded by so many professionals. At least she'd managed to get most of the dirt out from under her nails. The long, manicured tips of the women—some polished wives, a handful of firm partners—had her longing to hide her own.

She felt alive at Harrison's side, filled with pride as he introduced her, and nearly bursting with it as his associates regaled her with stories of his brilliance. He was well-liked and well-respected. A good man, as so many of them echoed. She was going to marry a good man. They left the party after several hours and Poppy slipped her heels off in the car, eager to give her feet a break. She was a tennis-shoes and ballet flats kind of woman. Back at his house, she changed into yoga pants and a long t-shirt, tucking the designer gown carefully back in the garment bag before walking out of the bathroom.

"Do you mind if we talk for a bit before you leave?"

Poppy checked the time; still early enough to stick around a bit. Harrison sat at one end of the couch and Poppy sat straight up on the edge of the armchair across the room. She couldn't get too comfortable, it would be a mistake. "What do you need?"

Fiona jumped up on Harrison's lap and he stroked her head and back. Poppy had never been so jealous of a cat before. Harrison scratched the cat's ears as he asked, "Do you think we should tell your family soon?"

Poppy twisted her opal ring around her thumb, "I don't know, Harrison. Dad is in the rehab center and Mom is practically killing herself trying to be two places at once. Andi is coming home this week for Christmas and we are just hoping that Dad gets to come home sometime soon. It's just not a good time," she wrapped up weakly.

Harrison rubbed a hand over his jaw, "I don't

know if there will ever be a really good time, Poppy. I mean, we are getting married next week and your family still doesn't know we are dating. Can't we at least tell them that?"

Poppy shook her head. "I'm just not ready to explain it all. I'm not even sure they will buy the whole dating story when I tell them, and if the whole story comes out, it still feels so crazy and impulsive. I'm kind of afraid of what they will do. Speaking of which, I'll try to give you a heads up, but I'm one hundred percent sure Hawthorne is going to hunt you down whenever he finds out, so... yeah."

Poppy stood and grabbed her duffel bag, "Look, I'll figure out when we can do it. But not right now, okay?"

Harrison stood and sighed. "Okay. I just sort of want everyone to know so we can stop this sneaking around." He tugged the duffel bag out of her hand and opened the front door for her. He walked her out to the truck and Poppy climbed in, then grabbed the bag from Harrison.

He leaned on the door, his breath freezing into puffs of steam in the chilly night air, and his face cast in dark shadows from the streetlight behind them. "Will I see you before the wedding?"

Poppy studied the outline of his face. "I don't think so. I need to be home."

"What about Christmas plans? Will I come to your house?" Poppy couldn't hide the wince and Harrison changed course, "Will you come to mine?" Christmas seemed like a long time from now, and Poppy still had no idea what it would look like for her family. Would dad be home? Would she be able to sneak away?

"I'm not sure. We can talk about it later, okay?"

Harrison nodded and shut the truck door, rapping his knuckle on the roof before stepping away and watching Poppy pull out of the drive. She looked back at Harrison standing on his driveway in navy sweatpants and a hooded sweatshirt. Was she crazy to wish that she could go sit on the couch with Fiona and Harrison, instead of returning to the same bedroom she'd had since returning home from college? It was cold in the truck, but she knew there would be warmth at Harrison's side. If only he wanted her there for more than his political aspirations.

12

Poppy stood nervously, her sweater-dress and boots suddenly too warm, despite the chilly air she'd walked through to get to the Vigo County Courthouse. Judge Romano, apparently another friend of Harrison, stood before them.

She fidgeted, brushing her hair out of her face, annoyed that she hadn't pulled it back in a braid. It didn't really matter what she wore or how she looked, it was just Harrison. Her wedding day and no one would be there. Growing up, she could have never imagined getting married without her sisters beside her. They used to play wedding and take turns being the bride and bridesmaids. Poor Hawthorne occasionally got roped into playing the groom!

Yet, the reality of today wasn't a line of sisters to

her left, each holding bouquets and standing in matching dresses. Instead, it was her and Harrison, and the judge.

Harrison pulled her aside, asking the judge for a moment.

"Are you okay?"

She nodded, meeting his eyes and hoping hers didn't betray her by spilling the tears that threatened. "This was what I want to do, I just didn't expect it to be this hard."

He smiled softly and pushed her hair back from her cheek, the tender gesture nearly undoing her. "We can call someone. One of your sisters?"

Poppy shook her head. "No, I'm okay. I'm ready." She took a deep breath and started to head back toward the judge. Harrison touched her arm and gently spun her back to him.

"Poppy?"

"Yes?"

"You look beautiful today," he said softly.

Unable to speak, she smiled and swiped at the moisture gathering in the corner of her eye. "Let's get this over with, Coulter."

Returning to the judge, Harrison squeezed Poppy's hand and gave her a warm smile.

The judge cleared his throat and turned to Harrison. "Okay, are we all ready?"

As Judge Romano began reading from a script, Poppy struggled to listen to his words.

"We are gathered here today to witness and to celebrate the decision of Harrison and Poppy to join themselves together in the union of marriage. Because of its importance, it should be entered into only with a deep sense of responsibility. Marriage is entered into reverently, or it is no marriage."

Was she doing the right thing? They were entering into this reverently, with no illusions that it wasn't the forever deal. But shouldn't they be in a church? Or at least with a pastor? Or someone who would pray for them?

The judge continued, "Harrison and Poppy, you now stand as two individuals, at the beginning of your life as one. Although your backgrounds and experiences are different, you share the same goals and ideals. Today, you stand here together on the threshold of a lifelong journey of friendship and love. And, as you take your first step in this great journey, you must remember that you are making the most serious commitment of your lives."

The threshold. Yes, it definitely felt like stepping

into something. Poppy felt like the adventurer stepping onto an invisible bridge, trusting that there was something there. Something that would grow into love. She had loved Harrison once and he hadn't even known. Could he love her enough for a lifetime?

"While this ceremony will formally unite you in marriage, only you can unite with each other in your hearts. If a relationship of mutual love and respect does not already exist between you, this ceremony cannot create that relationship."

Oh boy. Exactly how much had Harrison told Judge Romano about their situation? She glanced up from the spot on Harrison's shirt she'd been staring at to meet his eyes, which were locked on hers. His smile was confident and the skin around his eyes slightly wrinkled. He squeezed her hand again.

"In sharing the most intimate relationship of husband and wife there will be times of stress, sacrifice, and sorrow. May you face them together and overcome adversity with the same love, understanding, and faith in each other that you feel at this moment. Harrison and Poppy, of all the people you know, you have chosen each other as partners in your life's journey together.

"Do you Harrison solemnly declare in the presence of God and these witnesses that you take this woman, Poppy, whom you hold by your right hand to be your lawfully wedded wife?"

Poppy's heart lurched. She looked up and found her soon-to-be husband's dark brown eyes on hers, questions in their depths. What was he thinking?

Harrison quietly cleared his throat before responding, "I do."

"Do you promise to support her, love her, cherish her, protect her and care for her as long as you both shall live?"

"I do."

"Harrison, at this time, as you look into Poppy's eyes, I ask you to repeat after me." Judge Romano directed Harrison through the vows, Harrison's gaze remained locked on Poppy's, the muddy brown of his eyes reminding her of the creek after a heavy rain.

"Poppy, I take you as my wife. I pledge to share my life openly with you." He repeated the words slowly, and they sank down into her belly where an unfamiliar fire burned. "I promise to honor and tenderly care for you. I commit to cherish and encourage you for all the days of our lives."

Judge Romano turned to her. "Do you, Poppy, solemnly declare in the presence of God and these witnesses that you take this man, Harrison, whom you hold by your right hand to be your lawfully wedded husband?"

It was Poppy's turn to respond and she swallowed the lump forming in her throat before responding. "I do."

HARRISON WATCHED POPPY'S EYES, glistening with moisture from unfallen tears. Were they tears of joy? She repeated slowly after the judge. "Harrison, I take you as my husband. I pledge to share my life openly with you. I promise to honor and tenderly care for you and I commit to cherish and encourage you for all the days of our lives."

The judge held out his hand for the rings and Harrison pulled them from his pocket.

"You have brought here today two rings. These rings have neither a beginning nor an end. May they be a symbol of your everlasting love and fidelity. May they always remind you of the solemn vows and obligations you have taken today." As though Harrison would ever forget. When the judge directed him, Harrison placed the ring he'd picked for Poppy on her finger and repeated his final vows.

"With this ring, I take you as my wife and pledge

to you my love and fidelity as we join our lives together." Harrison felt the solemnity of the promise in every word. I pledge to you my love.

Poppy placed the heavy titanium band on his finger and she spoke the same words. "With this ring, I take you as my husband and pledge to you my love and fidelity as we join our lives together."

Judge Romano continued, "May these rings stand as a sign to you of your desire to live, love, to create, and to build your lives together. May you find your marriage a refuge in times of trouble. And may your hearts be united by your true affection for each other. For as much as you have consented together in marriage and have pledged your faith and love, by virtue of the authority vested in me by the state of Indiana, I now pronounce you husband and wife."

"Harrison, you may kiss your bride."

Harrison studied his wife. Wife. The word carried so much weight, all the promises he had just made before God to love and honor the woman across from him. Her hand in his was delicate, but strong. Callouses and short fingernails evidence of her hard-working spirit and love of the land.

He dropped her hand and reached for her, placing a hand gently on her waist and guiding her close, forcing her to lift her chin to maintain eye contact. Then, he lowered his head and watched as her eyes fell closed.

Under his, her lips were warm and soft, impossibly sweet. The whisper of a kiss was achingly brief, her fresh lemon scent surrounding him and he forced himself to pull back, even as every part of him was arguing to pull her closer and kiss her deeper.

Poppy was his wife, but they were not together. She didn't love him and he wasn't looking for passion. Still, as her eyes fluttered open and she smiled shyly at him, Harrison's heart raced and he couldn't help but grin back. This was the right thing, despite how crazy it seemed from the outside, he knew in his heart that God's hand was on this marriage.

He and Poppy stepped into the lobby of the courthouse. She looked up at him and asked, "So, uh, what do we do now?"

He shrugged. "I don't really know. I guess we just go back to work. Will you come to Christmas with my parents? I think Easton is going to come."

Poppy shook her head, "I can't miss Christmas at the farm." He tried not to let his disappointment show, but Poppy must read minds because she said, "I could come out for Christmas Eve?"

"Christmas Eve works great. I'll let Mom know."

Poppy twisted her new ring around her finger, a large solitaire diamond set in gold with smaller diamonds circling. "Okay. Wednesday night then."

Today was only Thursday, and a week seemed like a long time to wait to see her. "I feel like we should go have lunch or something. To celebrate."

Poppy laughed, "Celebrate alone?"

Harrison shrugged. "I don't know. It feels weird to go back to my office after getting married."

"Yeah, I guess it does." She wiggled the ring and Harrison rubbed his own with the pad of his thumb. "I could eat," she finally offered.

Poppy pulled off her wedding ring, tucking it safely in the glove box of her truck, and stepped back onto the familiar soil of Bloom's Farm. In the midst of the crazy changes taking place, Poppy was especially grateful for the solid, unchanging foundation of her family and the farm.

It felt like she had been praying nonstop since Harrison proposed, if you could technically call it a proposal. Still, she sent up another prayer. Somehow, she had to navigate how to tell her parents and her siblings about this. Hawthorne was going to flip out, protective as he was.

She hated that she couldn't tell them, but she definitely needed to lay the groundwork first. The plan to tell them at Thanksgiving had gotten derailed, and since then, the entire family had been in survival mode. Christmas, she could share that they were dating, and once her family warmed up to the idea, she would break the news that they were already married. Maybe it wasn't her best plan, but it was the only one she had right now.

Christmas Eve would be...interesting, to say the least. From what Harrison had said, his parents hadn't been exactly thrilled at the news that he was marrying her. He assured her it had nothing to do with her as a person, but was more about the circumstances of the arrangement. Still, she couldn't help but worry that his family wouldn't like her. What would they think of a woman who agreed to marry their son without a foundation of love?

Christmas Eve was a week away. So until then, she would focus on the farm.

Twisting her fingers around the now bare ring finger of her left hand, acutely aware of the ring that should be there, she walked to her office, hoping to avoid her family until she could get a better hold on hiding this secret. Secrets never lasted long in the Bloom Family, but this had to be different. Maybe it would be best to limit her time with them until Christmas.

Lavender would be the only problem, especially since she'd been full of questions since the Harvest Festival. But Lavender wasn't prone to gossip, and without hearing something directly from Poppy, her sister wouldn't share it with anyone else.

That night, Harrison texted her. **Goodnight, Mrs. Coulter.**

She replied quickly, with a smile on her face. **I'm still a Bloom, Senator. Did I ever actually agree to change my name?**

She was unsurprised when his name came up on the caller ID almost immediately.

"Well, hello, *husband*."

"You are going to change your name, right?" he asked with no segue.

She smiled, figuring she should let him squirm a little bit. "I don't know, Harrison," she said with mock seriousness, "I run Bloom's Farm, after all. Shouldn't I be Poppy Bloom?"

"I just assumed you would—" he sputtered.

"You know what they say about that," she countered. The silence stretched and Poppy stifled a giggle.

Harrison exhaled and said "You're just messing with me, aren't you?" The breath Poppy was holding burst out with a loud laugh.

"Yes, Harrison. I will change my name. Eventually," she added.

"Good. For this to work, people have to really believe we are in love." And there it was again: the glaring reminder that this marriage and this entire relationship wasn't real.

Her laughter subsided and she took on a more serious tone. "Are you sure we are doing the right thing?" Technically it was too late, but surely they could still annul the marriage. Wasn't that a thing?

"Poppy, would you mind if I prayed for us?" he asked, hesitantly. "I mean, I've been praying a lot by myself about this whole situation, but I feel like maybe it would help for us to pray together, you know?"

Her heart squeezed and she nodded, then laughed realizing he couldn't see her. "I would like that."

Harrison prayed, and as she listened to him ask for wisdom and guidance, she echoed it. When he asked for their friendship to deepen, she felt her eyes sting. He continued, thanking God for the ceremony that bound them together.

When he finished, Poppy couldn't speak.

"Are you still there?"

"Yep," she choked out. "I'm here. Thanks, Harrison. This is all still a bit crazy."

"It is. But it's going to work out. We will just take it slow."

He changed subjects, asking about the rest of her day. Poppy closed her bedroom door and paced her room as they spoke. There were too many ears in this house.

13

Harrison worked at his law office each day, Christmas Eve coming painfully slowly. During the legislative session, he would only be in the office one day a week and on the weekends. The rest of the year, Harrison worked in Terre Haute four days a week, reserving one day in Indianapolis for other meetings. Still, it was easy to get behind, and this time of year seemed busier than the rest, as everyone tried to get things done before the holidays.

He waited anxiously, pacing the entryway and looking out the window for Poppy's obnoxious truck. She needed something more appropriate, especially if she would be driving back and forth to Indianapolis for events and press conferences.

Harrison had offered to pick Poppy up at the farm, but she declined. He would spend the night at his parents, and Poppy would probably insist on going home. At least they weren't trying to fool his family. He hadn't told Easton yet. Easton would probably blame his parents for coming up with the crazy idea. Easton claimed the pressure to live up to the Coulter family name drove him to moving away and going off-grid, which Harrison thought was ridiculous. Their parents had high expectations, but didn't every parent?

It wasn't like his parents had pushed him to go into politics or even law school. His brother had rebelled against any expectations from their parents. But Harrison loved him. He wouldn't try to keep it a secret from his brother, which meant Poppy had no reason to spend the night. That was a bridge he wasn't ready to cross yet, anyway.

Finally, the rusty gray truck pulled into the drive, looking out of place against the well-trimmed landscape and pristine white gravel drive. He stepped onto the porch to greet her and grabbed her hand. Her ring finger was bare though, and he held it up to confirm. He frowned. "Where is your ring?"

"Oh, shoot. Just a second." He watched through

the passenger window as she dug in the glove box before hopping back out.

"You keep your wedding ring in the glove box?" he asked with a raised eyebrow. That ring was worth ten times more than the truck.

She blushed, "Sorry, I couldn't let anyone see me wearing it, and that seemed like the safest place."

He understood her reasoning, but it still chaffed. Did she not take the marriage as seriously as he did? Harrison had worn his ring all week. It actually made him smile when the flash of silver caught his eye while he flipped through a stack of legal briefs. But Poppy had buried hers in her grungy old truck. "Can I buy you a chain to wear it on?"

Poppy shook her head, "I'll figure it out. Eventually I'll be able to wear it normally, right?"

"Right," he agreed, but eventually seemed like a long time. She hadn't even told her family they were dating. "Well, let's go in. Mom is excited to meet you." Of course, for the regal Marilyn Coulter, that meant she had hired a team of professionals to clean the house and ordered catering for dinner in addition to the traditional Christmas meal for tomorrow. Plus, she was currently putting on her best display of domesticity by pulling fresh-baked cookies from the oven. The dough had been store-bought, but Marilyn was all about the optics. Actually, his mother would make a pretty good political adviser. She and Neil got along wonderfully.

They went inside and into the kitchen. "Mom, I'd like you to meet Poppy Bloom. My wife," he added. His mother's eyebrows went straight to her hairline.

"Oh, well. Poppy," his mother crooned, "it's lovely to meet you. Harrison told us you were... engaged, but this is a surprise."

Poppy blushed, "I'm sorry we held the wedding without you, Mrs. Coulter. I hope you'll help me plan a big reception when we make the news public."

His mother beamed at the invitation, and Harrison gave Poppy a grateful smile. How had she known the way to his mother's heart would be through a party?

"Come in, come in. Take off your coat. Would you like a cookie, dear?"

His dad shuffled in, warming his hands near the stove and snagging a cookie from the plate Harrison's mom held out to Poppy.

"Dad, this is Poppy," Harrison said.

"Harrison's wife," his mother added pointedly.

His father grunted and flashed Harrison a look

that meant they would talk about this later. "Nice to meet you, Poppy." He ran a hand over his beard, "Welcome to the family, I suppose."

"Thank you," Poppy said quietly. Harrison saw the trepidation on her face and he stepped close, laying a hand on her shoulder.

"Easton said he would be here around five. Did he tell you?"

His mom brightened, "No, he didn't say anything. Oh, I'll be so glad to have you both home for a few days." Then his mom looked at his dad, wrinkled her nose, and said, "Why don't you go clean up, Reggie? You smell like cows."

Harrison hid a smile behind a bite of cookie and his dad trudged out of the room. It felt good to be home, and surprisingly normal to have Poppy there with him. Hopefully Easton wouldn't ruin it.

Poppy sat at the elegant dining table, with a centerpiece that would rival anything used to decorate the most lavish weddings at Storybook Barn. Poppy didn't usually find herself feeling self-conscious, but this stilted family dinner was far removed from the usual banter and chaos of family dinners at the

Bloom household. The tension was making her skin crawl.

Easton arrived late and Marilyn insisted on holding dinner for him. Poppy could see the similarity in the brothers, despite Easton's tanned skin and sun-bleached hair. They had the same strong jawline, although Harrison's was clean-shaven, while his brother's wore several days of scruff.

A whirlwind of energy, Easton entered the house with a loud "Whoop!" He wrapped Harrison in a big hug before pulling him under his armpit to press his knuckle into his younger brother's scalp. Poppy watched, dumbfounded, as the distinguished senator and her well-dressed, always calm and collected husband turned into a twelve-year-old boy before her eyes.

Marilyn rolled her eyes and gave a motherly yell that told Poppy she'd definitely encountered this chaos before. Then, Easton spotted Poppy and gave Harrison a side-eyed glance.

"And who is this lovely lady? Surely, you aren't here with my uptight little brother?" Poppy blushed and looked at Harrison, who glared at his brother.

"She's taken," Harrison commented.

"Oh, come on now, I don't see a—" Easton held

up Poppy's hand and his jaw dropped, "ring." He finished weakly. "Seriously, bro?"

Harrison scoffed, "Yeah, seriously, *bro.* What are you, twenty-one?"

"I just never expected to come home and find you tied the knot and didn't even let me know." Easton glanced at Poppy and added, "No offense."

Reggie came downstairs and Easton straightened, his warm smile and boisterous persona disappearing into stiff formality. "Dad."

"Easton. I'm, ahem, glad you made it home."

"Sure," he replied. The tension surrounded Poppy like a heavy morning fog on the farm, and she gave a concerned glance to Harrison. He shook his head slightly. Apparently, this was a family issue, and for now, Poppy wasn't family, despite the ring on her finger.

The evening remained stilted, though flashes of Easton's vivacious personality showed up occasionally, mostly as he laughed and flirted with Poppy.

"You know, my sailboat has an extra cabin. We can literally sail off into the sunset together," he wiggled his eyebrows at her and Poppy couldn't help but laugh.

"Easton! That's enough," Reggie barked, his agitation at his eldest son evident.

"What? I'm just having a little fun!"

Poppy ducked her head as they continued arguing. "Flirting with your brother's wife is inappropriate, Easton James," Reggie scolded.

Harrison tried to steer the conversation in a different direction. "How's the charter business, Easton? Met anyone interesting lately?"

"My job is the best, seriously." Reggie scoffed and Marilyn shot her husband a look of disapproval. "People come from all over the world, and I get to talk with them and show them the beauty of the ocean. Plus, I spend all day sailing and all night in my hammock."

Harrison asked, "Don't you ever get tired of wearing swim trunks?"

Poppy could see the appeal, but couldn't help but ask, "Don't you miss your family and friends?"

Easton shook his head. "Sure, I miss some people," Poppy didn't miss the way his eyes moved toward his father, "but putting on real pants to fly here was a pretty big bummer, for real."

Everyone laughed, except Reggie, who pushed back from the table. He spoke to his wife, "Dinner was delicious, dear. I'm going to go lie down for a bit."

Whatever the history was between Reggie and

Easton, it was seriously uncomfortable. Even more uncomfortable than she expected her own marriage announcement to be. Most of her sisters knew of her past with Harrison, and how she'd skipped her own prom in disappointment. They weren't likely to forgive Harrison easily.

After dinner, Poppy and Harrison cleared the table while Easton regaled them with stories of the scuba divers he'd taken out the week before. One woman had gotten sea sick climbing back into the boat, a story that ended with her emptying the contents of her stomach onto her new husband as he followed her.

With their father gone, the atmosphere loosened up. It was obvious Marilyn desperately missed her son, but that she wouldn't push him or convey her disappointment about his living so far away. She dropped a few hints about how wonderful it would be to see him more often.

They played cards after the dishes were done and Poppy watched the interaction of Harrison and his brother with interest.

"So, when was the wedding? And where was my invitation?"

Harrison cleared his throat. "Um, actually it was

last Thursday. And we eloped. Nobody was invited, so don't feel left out."

"You eloped? Mister Strategize-to-Death? No way."

Harrison shrugged. "It's true."

Easton looked at Poppy, "And you were okay with that? No wedding party or fancy dress? You could have had a destination wedding on the beach. I get a lot of those. I could probably get you a sweet deal with my friend in Jamaica. Harrison, what are you thinking?"

Poppy laughed, "It was fine, I promise. I don't need an expensive dress or imported flowers." Harrison had gotten her two expensive dresses already. Of course, she'd only worn one of them.

Harrison's smile didn't reach his eyes, "See, Easton, it was fine."

"A girl doesn't dream about her wedding day being fine, bro. It's supposed to be magical." He traced his hand in front of him in the shape of a rainbow with a goofy look on his face. Then, he dropped his hands and asked, "What was the hurry, anyway? You're not... you know." He glanced meaningfully at her stomach and her mouth fell open.

Harrison jumped up, "Okay, Easton, that's about

enough. You will not insult my wife any further. I love you and I'm glad you are home, but if you so much as look at her sideways again, we will be done." Harrison poked a finger in his brother's shoulder, "Got it?"

"Whoa, whoa. I was just asking! You have to admit, this isn't exactly normal Harrison-the-Great behavior!"

Poppy hated seeing the two of them argue, and she jumped in before Harrison could, laying her hand on his. "Easton, it's not what you think." She looked at their hands, joined and pulled them a part. "We aren't..." How should she explain? "We got married so Harrison can run for governor."

Easton's mouth dropped open and his eyes closed. "Of course you did. Are you out of your mind, Harrison?"

Harrison bristled. "It's my life, East. You think I'm the crazy one? You are the one who quit your job as an engineer to go be a beach bum! At least I'm trying to do something with my life and make the world a little better." Oh boy, this was not going well.

"Wow. Okay. Tell me how you really feel, Harrison."

Harrison deflated, rubbing his jaw with his right hand. "Ugh. I'm sorry, I'm just tired of defending my choices. Mom and Dad weren't thrilled about this either, but Poppy and I made the decision and we feel like it was the right one."

Easton's gazed dropped to their joined hands again. "Maybe. Or else you are just fooling yourselves. Mark my words, Harrison. This is going to end one of two ways. Either you two fall in love, or you break each other's hearts."

Harrison dropped her hand as though it had burned him, and Poppy's heart sank, realizing perhaps the most likely scenario was a combination of the two.

14

Poppy sat next to Lily on the couch, claiming seniority and kicking Rose to the floor with Lavender. Mom was in the kitchen prepping dinner, and while Poppy had been helping for a while, she was taking a little break to enjoy a cup of coffee and watch whatever cheesy Hallmark movie Rose had turned on.

No surprise that Daisy was sitting practically on top of Andi, who had been home for about a week. While Dandelion was gone, Poppy and Daisy were closer, but as soon as her twin returned, Daisy tended to latch on. Her sister didn't do it intentionally, but sometimes Poppy felt like the second choice.

Dad sat next to her on the couch, silent and observing, instead of his usual booming laughter and vivacious spirit. Poppy laid a hand on his leg, surprised how small he felt under the goofy reindeer pajama pants Lavender had bought him.

It was definitely not the typical Bloom family Christmas, with her mom decking the halls of the main house with garland and lights. Rose and Lavender had helped Lily put up the tree a few days ago. They'd texted Poppy to help, but she'd been out Christmas shopping, trying to figure out what in the world she was supposed to get for her secret husband. This whole situation was far too complicated.

Her mom's voice interrupted the Christmas movie and chatter. "Dinner's ready!" Hawthorne and Avery, his girlfriend, led the group into the dining room. Poppy stood to the side as Rose lingered behind to help their dad move from the couch to the table.

When Hawthorne finished praying, they started passing dishes around the table. Brunch used to be a weekly occurrence for their family. Instead of missing it, Poppy was grateful they hadn't been happening, because it meant fewer chances for her to accidentally let something slip about Harrison. Then she felt guilty for wishing away family time.

Daisy spoke over the clanging of dishes and

requests for salt and pepper. "You know, we need to start up Saturday brunches now that Dad is back home," Daisy said.

Lavender and Lily chimed in with their agreement, but Poppy bit her tongue. She was enjoying the family time, but how long could she keep up the act?

"Yeah, I know we all live and work around her, but I still miss you guys," Hawthorne said.

Poppy loved teasing Hawthorne, and she didn't miss the opportunity to needle him for that particular comment. "Awww! Girls, did you hear that? He likes us! He *really* likes us!" Poppy folded her hands together in front of her chest, acting overly excited. It felt so good to be with her entire family again. She watched as Daisy and Andi divided a giant cinnamon roll, each taking half with unspoken agreement. Rose and Hawthorne teased back and forth as Avery looked on with amusement. Her father was quiet, but his drooping smile and a shaky hand patted her mother's where it rested on the table. Yes, her family and this farm meant everything to her. But the shadow of the secret she kept hovered over the table and darkened her mood. She needed to tell her family, but when?

After dinner, she asked Andi downstairs. If

anyone in their family could keep a secret, it was Andi. None of them really knew what Andi did, but it had to do with security for the General who oversaw the deployed troops. Keeping secrets meant saving lives for Andi.

And Poppy was dying to tell someone.

"Okay, Andi. I promise I'm going to tell everyone soon, but for now, can you keep a secret?"

Pacing around her bedroom, Poppy spilled everything to her most logical, unemotional sister. How she was worried about the farm, how Harrison had suggested a marriage that would help both of them. And how she was afraid she might fall in love with him. Andi watched, her face betraying none of her thoughts until Poppy finished. "So, what do you think?"

Andi ran a hand over her blonde pixie cut. "I think you should go upstairs and tell everyone."

Poppy threw up her hands, "I can't do that! Everyone will think I'm crazy!"

"Maybe you are, Pop. This is quite a pickle you've gotten into. I guess I can understand why you thought you needed to do it, but I think there is more to it than you say. There were other ways to help the farm."

Poppy frowned and fiddled with the empty

space where her wedding ring should be. "What do you mean?"

"I mean, I think you wanted to say yes to Harrison because of how you feel about him."

Her denial was adamant, and she shook her head. "I'm over him. He humiliated me."

"I know," Andi acknowledged, "but that was a long time ago. I'm just saying from everything you've told me, this had more to do with you and Harrison than it did the farm." Andi's intelligent green eyes seemed to see straight through Poppy.

Poppy finally sat next to her sister on the bed, "What do I do now?"

"Keep praying, I guess. Maybe this was God's plan all along, I don't know. But keeping the secret is tearing you up, Pop." Andi drew her in for a hug.

"Thanks, Andi. I really miss you, you know."

"I miss you, too."

Poppy would tell them that she was dating Harrison. Soon.

15

Two weeks later, when Poppy asked him for a favor, Harrison was in Indianapolis for the start of the legislative session. This session would be crucial for him to establish himself as a serious candidate for governor by making a big impact and introducing key legislation.

But Poppy hadn't asked him for much, and this was a small favor, too. He glanced at his watch, just a few minutes late. Perfect. Harrison did love to make an entrance. This little visit would be fun. Poppy's sister, Daisy, was having trouble with the inspector from the county – bogus complaints and unreasonable inspections. With a little digging, he knew exactly why.

He scheduled his meeting with Gerald Ruiz, the

county commissioner, to start fifteen minutes before Poppy said she and Daisy would arrive. When he entered the county offices, Harrison was escorted directly back to the commissioner's office.

Mr. Ruiz was kind, eager to be helpful and make an ally of the senator from the district. Harrison humored the man, complimenting the county and his leadership. Then, he briefly mentioned the meeting happening across the building and invited the commissioner to join him.

As they walked, Harrison continued their chat. "I definitely want to hear more about the new Business and Education Partnership, Commissioner." He checked his watch again and stepped aside to allow Mr. Ruiz to open the conference room door. Perfect. "That sounds like an excellent project that would be beneficial across the entire state."

Harrison's eyes immediately found Poppy's in the small conference room, and he smiled. He saw the shock and confusion on Daisy Bloom's face and gave her a nod.

He looked down at the man Poppy had described to him over the phone, "You must be Mr. Havershem, the inspector. I'm Senator Harrison Coulter from the 83rd district."

The man stammered and Harrison looked back

toward his new friend, Mr. Ruiz, who was introducing himself to Daisy and greeting Poppy, whom he already knew. The commissioner exhorted the county's commitment to local businesswomen like themselves.

Daisy nodded, "Thank you, sir. Unfortunately, the process hasn't included as much... support from the county as I'd hoped." She glared across the table at the inspector.

Harrison watched with amusement as the commissioner questioned his employee. When Mr. Havershem started to deny and deflect, Harrison cut in. "From my understanding, your inspector has been intentionally placing roadblocks to prevent Miss Bloom here from successfully completing her project. As someone deeply involved in the Indiana Senate Committee for Economic Development, I have to say this is very disappointing. Small businesses are the heart of the economy and we should do everything in our power to aid," he glanced at Mr. Havershem, "not hinder, their progress."

Ruiz nodded enthusiastically, voicing his avid agreement. He questioned the inspector again when Daisy and Poppy started to explain about bogus complaints against the bed-and-breakfast and unfair targeting by Mr. Havershem.

Harrison laid a hand on Poppy's shoulder, seeing the fire rising in her eyes. Harrison had the ace-in-the-hole. Someone who messed with his wife's family was messing with him.

"I had my people do a little digging, and I am confident that there has been an egregious conflict of interest on the part of Mr. Havershem."

At Harrison's words, the inspector spewed a story filled with his hatred at Daisy. Poppy lunged in his direction. Despite her size, Poppy was feisty. He laid a hand on her arm and spoke over the clash of shouts and accusations. "Enough!"

The room fell silent as everyone waited to see what he had to say and Harrison reveled in the sense of power. "Everybody, sit," he commanded.

He pulled a chair out for Poppy, figuring that was the only way she would listen. Everyone else might follow his orders, but Poppy? She was a fifty-fifty chance at best. Harrison turned to the commissioner and spoke firmly, "Gerald, for the sake of Bloom's Farm's success as a multi-dimensional farm tourism attraction, we need the county to unsuspend the work permits for Bloom's Farm B&B. And for the projects currently suspended under the contractor..." He glanced at Daisy, "what's his name again?"

"Lance Matthews Construction," she responded.

"Right. Matthews. He was also unfairly targeted by Larry in an ill-advised attempt to damage the reputation and progress of Bloom's Farm B&B. We also expect the county will take appropriate disciplinary actions against Mr. Havershem for his gross misconduct in this regard."

Larry, the inspector, tried to speak, but the commissioner held up a hand to silence him, "We will discuss this later. Mr. Coulter—"

"Senator." Harrison corrected the commissioner as a reminder to everyone in the room.

The commissioner apologized and confirmed everything would be cleared up right away. Exactly as Harrison had hoped. He checked his watch again. Time to go, he had a meeting at the capital tonight.

He walked out with Poppy and her sister. When Daisy thanked him, he flashed her a smile, "It's my pleasure, truly."

He glanced at Poppy and then his watch again, "I'm sorry, but I really do have to run." Harrison leaned in to kiss her cheek and whispered in her ear, "That was fun. Call me later, beautiful." Then he turned and walked back toward his car, pulling his phone to his ear to call Bethany. It was going to be a long night.

~

Poppy watched Harrison walk away and felt the lingering whisper of his cheek against hers. He had been exactly what she needed him to be in that meeting. That confident, almost-condescending politician who knew exactly what he wanted and how to make it happen. It had been amazing to watch, even if he might have enjoyed the power trip a little too much. She'd have to be sure to humble him a bit later.

Daisy practically dragged her back to the truck, and Poppy stared at the steering wheel, avoiding her sister's gaze.

"Anything you need to tell me, sis?"

There was no going back now, not after Harrison had practically broadcast their status during the entire meeting, and then on the sidewalk outside. She turned to Daisy and tried to explain, "I meant to tell you a long time ago. Then Dad had his stroke and everything got complicated."

Daisy frowned, "So, what is it?"

"Harrison and I are...together." There, that was true. Not entirely inclusive, but still not a lie.

Her sister gasped dramatically. "Are you serious?" At Poppy's small nod, Daisy covered her mouth. "When?"

Poppy stretched the truth a bit but explained that Harrison had called her and they started dating. Technically true, if the event for IOSFA counted as a date.

"But you like him?"

Way too much, actually. Poppy nodded, "Yeah. I think you'll be seeing him around a lot more." Poppy winced when Daisy let out a squeal and pulled her in for an uncomfortable hug across the center console.

Daisy sat back and considered her sister. "Thanks for calling in a favor from your influential *boyfriend.*"

Poppy laughed, "You are welcome. And he's not that influential." At least not yet. The good news was that by telling Daisy, Poppy had effectively told the entire family that she was with Harrison.

16

Harrison hung up the phone and ran a hand over his jaw. Senator Hawkins was being especially annoying today. It was six weeks into the legislative session and getting into the nitty gritty of everything that needed to happen. A heavy knock sounded and Neil came storming in.

"It's been two months, Harrison. When are you going to tell the world that you are married?"

Harrison raised his eyebrows at Neil's outburst. "Good to see you, too. Have a seat." Had it really been two months since the wedding? He glanced at his calendar. It was almost March.

"Not today, Coulter," Neil responded as he paced the office. "Bethany just got word from

Senator Blake's office that he is planning a run for Governor next year."

Interesting. Harrison hadn't heard anything, but it wasn't unusual for Bethany's extensive contacts throughout the senate to hear rumors long before he did. "Calm down, Neil. We knew there would be competition."

Neil threw his hands in the air. "Yes, we knew there would be competition. But I was expecting Rudding or Planks. Out of touch mayors or an unknown Joe Schmoe. Not the majority leader!" Harrison kicked his feet up on the desk while his friend rubbed his palms together, like he often did when he thought. "We've got to get out ahead of this. We need you and Poppy to go public and embrace the role of Indiana's most lovable couple. Popperson or whatever."

Harrison winced at the moniker. "Poppy's not ready, Neil. We've talked about this! Her family knows we are together, but just that we are dating. What's the hurry? We don't have to officially announce candidacy until late this year!"

Neil gave him an exasperated look. "You're right. We don't have to officially announce until later. But we do need to get your flagship donors on board.

And to do that, we need you and Poppy to be official and believable!"

Harrison held up a hand, "Okay, okay. I'll see what I can do to push the timeline with Poppy, but it's not so simple for her. This is her entire life, Neil. And you need to calm down before you have another heart attack." Neil had a heart attack last summer, the likely result of too many steak dinners and too much stress.

His friend and confidant took a deep breath, and Harrison stood to escort him out. Neil stammered objections at the dismissal. At the threshold of the door, Neil looked back, "If you don't do something about this soon, I will. Okay, Harrison?"

"Yeah, yeah. It's going to be fine, Neil." Harrison nudged him out the door and shut it behind him. Neil was always extra worked up about something or other, but the man knew what he was talking about. If he said they needed to go public sooner, rather than later, he would do his best to make it happen.

Still, he hated to pressure Poppy. He'd sort of rushed her into this whole situation and it seemed unfair to push her more. They were in a surprisingly good place right now, with chats on the phone and a few cozy evenings at his Terre Haute residence that he enjoyed more than he probably should.

If Poppy needed a few more weeks to tell her family, he would give them to her.

FRIDAY NIGHT WAS the test run for Daisy's bed-and-breakfast, and the whole family was going to celebrate. Harrison invited Poppy over to watch a movie, but she turned him down. While he was busy in Indianapolis, it was easy to pretend they really were just dating. She rarely saw him, and her wedding ring remained firmly buried in the glove box of her truck.

On Wednesday before the party, Poppy caught up with Daisy. "Are you excited for the big day?"

Daisy nodded. "I think so. I will be fixing breakfast instead of Bonnie, because she had already planned to have her grandkids this weekend. But I don't think Jacquie or Mandy will mind."

Daisy's godmother, Jacquie, was an investor in the bed-and-breakfast and would be one of the first guests. Their friend, Mandy, and her husband were the others. Poppy smiled, "No, I'm sure Mandy and Garrett will be too preoccupied with having a weekend away from Adelaide." Garrett's five-year-old adopted niece was a joy, but Poppy knew Mandy had been looking forward to a little escape.

Daisy glanced at Poppy, "Is Harrison coming to the party?"

Poppy's eyes widened, she hadn't even considered inviting him. "Um, no, probably not. I'm sure he's had a long week," she deflected.

Daisy narrowed her eyes, "Are you guys still dating? How come I haven't heard anything else, or seen him around?"

"He came out to the farm right after Dad's stroke, but the senate is in session right now, and he's back and forth between here and Indianapolis all the time."

"But you still like him?"

Poppy reached for the empty spot on her ring finger, then caught herself and twisted the simple opal she wore on her thumb instead. "I really do."

Daisy nodded, "Then bring him along. It's time the rest of the family knew about you two."

"I'll see what I can do," Poppy said, even though she knew she wouldn't bring Harrison. She would tell everyone soon. Just not this weekend. It was Daisy's time to be in the spotlight, it was her party after all. "Oh, I did want to talk to you about the appetizers for the party," she said to Daisy.

Since Bonnie couldn't cater the party, Poppy had volunteered. With that, Daisy's questions about Harrison were forgotten.

Two weeks passed, and Poppy was no closer to telling her family. It was easy to find excuses not to. Avery and Hawthorne came home from Colorado, engaged and bursting with excitement for the big day and trying to set a date. It was mid-March, and Harrison was knee deep in the regular session, which had to wrap up by the end of April. They would have to reveal the extent of the relationship soon, and Poppy was dreading it. She didn't regret marrying Harrison, quite the opposite, actually. The moments she spent with Harrison, at his Christmas party, at his house or at a rare event in Indianapolis—they were a bright spot in her life right now.

Today, she was planting the last round of tomato seeds for their summer crops, which would start in the greenhouse. Her phone vibrated, surprising her because the greenhouse didn't have the most reliable cell reception. On the screen, there was a text message from Lavender.

Why wouldn't you tell me?

She must know about Harrison. But how had she found out?

Then, she saw the rest of her unread messages, a

string of text messages from people she rarely talked with.

Congratulations!

What a catch, can't believe you eloped!

Poppy closed her eyes as the phone continued to buzz in her palm, and notifications appeared in rapid fire across the screen. Whatever had happened was far bigger than her family.

Harrison's name and picture appeared on her screen with an incoming call. "Harrison, what is going on?"

"I'm so sorry, Poppy. I don't know how they found out."

Her mind raced through the options and she closed her eyes to ask the question she was dreading. "Who knows?"

Harrison hesitated and Poppy's heart sank. "Everybody, Poppy. Everyone knows about us. A reporter at the Indy Star ran a feature piece on me and somehow found out about the wedding. I don't know if it was court documents or what."

"It was in the newspaper?"

"I wish that was all. The TV station picked it up too, a human-interest piece on how romantic it was that we had a secret wedding and have kept the relationship out of the public eye while we enjoyed the honeymoon phase."

Poppy groaned, "This is a nightmare. Tell me I'm dreaming."

Harrison sighed, "Honestly, it could have been so much worse. They could have spun it as dishonest and reprehensible. At least right now, it seems like they are buying the whole whirlwind romance story."

Fantastic. "Yeah, well. They might buy it, but I don't think my family will."

"I'm sorry, Poppy. It wasn't supposed to happen like this."

17

Harrison walked up the steps to the main house at Bloom's Farm, full of nerves. The small bouquet he brought for Poppy's mother seemed trite and comically unimportant in light of what was about to happen. He felt like Daniel entering the lion's den.

Poppy's entire family had been blindsided with the news this week that Poppy was married—to someone they just found out she was dating two months ago. Probably because she wasn't actually dating him. Was it dating when you had movie night with the person you were married to, even if the marriage was a secret, and in name only?

Still, the Bloom family was tight-knit and Harrison was well aware that he was the cause of whatever rift this situation might cause. When he talked to Poppy, his main question had been about whether she wanted to let them believe they were in love or if she wanted to tell them the whole story.

The only problem was, the more people who knew about the marriage, the harder it was to keep the whole thing under wraps.

Harrison took a deep breath and knocked on the door, sending up a quick prayer as he waited for it to open. An older woman opened the door with a kind smile. "Harrison, please come in."

He held out the cheery bouquet, "These are for you, ma'am."

"Oh, how lovely. Please, call me Laura. After all, I suppose you are family, now."

Harrison's cheeks burned at the subtle reminder of their deceit, and he nodded and followed his mother-in-law into the house.

"You're a few minutes early, and most of my kids are still finishing up the morning chores before brunch. Why don't you come have a seat and talk with Keith and me?"

Harrison swallowed heavily. Where was Poppy? This felt a bit like an ambush. Still, he'd faced worse. And what parent wouldn't be pleased that their daughter had married a successful lawyer and public servant?

Keith was seated at the dining table already, a blanket over his lap. Harrison concealed his surprise at Poppy's father's appearance. He remembered Keith Bloom from community and school events over the years, but the man at the table was a far cry from the big, imposing impression he carried. Keith smiled at him and Harrison held out a hand. "Nice to see you again, Mr. Bloom."

Keith spoke slowly, his speech still slightly slurred. "Nice to see you, Harri-Harrison."

Laura offered him a cup of coffee and Harrison sat where he could see Laura while she fixed brunch and still see Keith. The silence settled uncomfortably in the kitchen, and Harrison again bemoaned the lack of Poppy's presence.

He cleared his throat, "I, uh, imagine you have some questions."

Laura raised her eyebrows and nodded. "You could say that." She glanced at Keith and then continued cutting up a cantaloupe. "We are trying to give grace, but I'll be honest and say we were very surprised and hurt to find out our daughter was married and hiding it from us." She scooped up the fruit with her knife and hand and tossed it into a bowl.

"We've already talked with Poppy, but we asked everyone to come late to brunch today so we could speak with you privately."

Ah, that explained the surprising lack of Bloom siblings in the house this morning.

"I'm very sorry that we didn't tell you sooner." He glanced at Keith, whose expression was guarded, "We got married just before Christmas, but I think she felt guilty and didn't want to add any more to the already full plate of the family."

Laura paused and pressed a hand towel to her eyes. "I guess I'm just still confused. She's been living here. We just thought you were dating?"

Harrison stood and stepped closer to his mother-in-law. "I'm very sorry, Mrs. Bloom. It was never our intention to hurt anyone. It seemed simpler for her to live at the farm, especially while I was in Indianapolis for the senate session so much.

"I care for your daughter very much, and I cannot wait to start our lives together in a home we share. But we know the wedding happened quickly, and we are willing to take everything else as slowly as needed. Poppy does not want to leave the farm or abandon the family. We weren't trying to make it more difficult for everyone else."

Laura nodded and picked up her knife. Harrison felt lucky the Blooms were a Christian family, and he likely didn't have to worry about an interrogation at knifepoint.

A door on the other side of the kitchen opened, and a man around Harrison's age walked in. Take that last thought back. Hawthorne might be the exception to that knifepoint comment.

"Hey, Mom. Why did we have to wait for—" Hawthorne spotted him standing next to his mother and froze, his jaw tightening. Harrison's brother-in-law set down a small basket of eggs on the counter. He had to admire Hawthorne's self-control, since by the looks of it, he was far more tempted to chuck them at Harrison than eat them for breakfast. "Awfully brave of you to show up for a family brunch."

"Hawthorne." Laura Bloom's voice held warning.

Not one to back down, Harrison replied, "Actually, I was invited. But I do wish we were meeting under better circumstances." He extended his hand to Hawthorne and a prayer to heaven.

Hawthorne glanced down at his hand and then back up to Harrison's face. "You mean the circumstances where you seduce my sister and secretly marry her without telling her family or anyone she cares about?"

Harrison cleared his throat, his face hot at the mention of seduction. "Again, I'm very sorry that we didn't tell anyone. It was not our intention to—"

A voice from behind him rang out, "Where is everyone? I thought I would be the last..." The woman's voice trailed off as Harrison turned around, and he saw a beautiful woman, slightly older than Poppy but with the same eyes. Lily. As she recognized him, her gaze cooled significantly, and she tilted her chin up. She glanced at Hawthorne, "I assume this is the guy?"

Hawthorne nodded. Harrison swallowed heavily. Where on earth was Poppy?

Lily stepped close and poked him with a finger. "I don't know what you did to make Poppy do something so reckless, but—"

"Lily!" Poppy's voice interrupted, and Harrison very nearly sagged in relief. "That's enough."

Poppy walked up to him and took his hand in hers, turning them so they could see the small crowd. Such strength in the face of what seemed to be a very angry firing squad. Of course, it was him they wanted to string up by his toenails. She was their sister.

"Poppy, what on earth? Why did you—"

Laura Bloom held up a hand, "Everybody just hang on. We will wait for everyone to get here so we only have to hash this out once. In the meantime," she gestured to the kitchen, "get some coffee, someone scramble some eggs, and remember that we don't live on the set of a reality TV show."

Harrison squeezed Poppy's hand, "Boy, am I glad to see you."

She gave him a reassuring smile, "It's going to be okay."

He wasn't so sure though. Only two siblings were here, and he already felt like he'd taken a beating. Which sisters were left?

Just then, Lavender came in, carrying a laptop. At last, a friendly face. Except, when she looked at him, he didn't see the encouraging smiles he had gotten at the Harvest Festival. She ignored him and spoke to the group. "I've got Andi on audio. Her video connection is too slow, but she wanted to listen in."

Great. Even the sister on the other side of the world didn't want to miss whatever was about to unfold here. He'd been scared of Poppy's parents?

No, the Bloom siblings were the hurdle he hadn't anticipated. How was he supposed to win them over?

He whispered in Poppy's ear, "Still sticking to the plan?"

She nodded and fingered his wedding ring. "Yes." She'd said on the phone last night that a story about a whirlwind romance was the most believable. He just hoped they weren't making another mistake by misleading everyone.

He stood by Poppy, who took a seat at a barstool as they sipped their coffee. Others chatted with Andi or helped fix breakfast. Daisy came in a few minutes later. "Sorry, everyone. I wanted to say goodbye to the guests before I headed over."

The youngest sister entered last, walking through the garage entrance. She removed her baseball hat and rolled up the sleeves of her plaid shirt.

Lily spoke first, "Okay, everyone is here now. I still don't know why we had to eat late."

"Your father and I wanted a chance to meet and speak with Harrison alone, without you pack of wolves circling."

"And?" Hawthorne asked.

Poppy stood. "Okay, everybody just chill for a second. I have a few things to say."

Harrison waited, eager as anyone to see how this was going to go.

Poppy took his hand again. "Harrison and I got married just before Christmas." A chorus of questions arose from the kitchen and Poppy shook her head, "Just listen! We had been seeing each other for a few months, and it was a crazy time for our family. With Harrison needing to go back to Indianapolis nearly full time during the senate session, it didn't seem necessary for me to move out just yet. At the time, it seemed like the right thing to do was have a quiet ceremony to start our life together and tell everyone later. I realize now," her voice rose again to cover the words of her siblings, "that it was a mistake to keep it from you. Harrison and I are very excited to build our life together, and we very much hope you can forgive us. If you want to be mad at anyone, please, be angry with me—not Harrison. He wanted to tell you from the beginning, but I resisted, afraid you would judge me as impulsive and foolish. But, I can assure you, I went into this marriage—we both did—with a clear head and having weighed all the options."

"Are you pregnant?" Daisy asked. At the shocked looks from the rest of the family Daisy looked around, "What? Shotgun wedding and none of you were thinking it?"

Harrison was offended on Poppy's behalf, but she only wore an amused smile, "Come on, Daisy. You know me better than that."

Hawthorne grumbled, "It's not *your* moral character I'm worried about."

"I'm not pregnant! Geesh." Poppy glanced at him, her eyes unreadable, "I'm not pregnant, but do look forward to having a family with Harrison. I love him very much."

Harrison's gut clenched at the declaration. Was this all an act? Was Poppy really that talented a storyteller? Because every word rang with sincerity, and the emotion he read on her face had him convinced it was real. But surely it was all for show, just to reassure her family. She couldn't love him, could she?

And if she did, what on earth was he going to do about it?

18

After Poppy gave her explanation to the family, things settled down a bit. She hadn't exactly planned on declaring her love for Harrison, but everything she said to her family was true. Harrison had covered his shock well, but she'd seen it on his face. The plan had been to avoid telling straight out lies to her family. Stretching the truth or lies of omission were gray areas she didn't want to examine too closely.

She sat at the table and watched as Harrison worked his charm on her family. When Poppy had said Harrison wanted to tell them immediately, she'd seen Hawthorne loosening his grip on his coffee cup and Lily relax her stance. Even Andi had only given him a mild warning before logging off saying, "If you hurt her, I will make you regret it."

Hawthorne had muttered something about a thousand acres being a lot of ground to search for a body, and Harrison had given her a wide-eyed look.

"Hawthorne, enough," Lavender had chimed in.

Since then, things at brunch were relatively normal, although much of the usual teasing was absent.

Poppy looked around, surprised to see one person surprisingly absent. "Where's Avery?" Lance wasn't here either, but Daisy promised to bring him next week.

"Her sister flew out for a visit. They are wedding dress shopping this morning."

Daisy squealed and Poppy felt a twinge of envy. She would never go wedding dress shopping with her sisters.

"Have you set a date?" Lily asked, reaching for her ever-present binder, where she organized all the events at Storybook Barn.

"Has anyone taken the second weekend in September?" Hawthorne asked. "Her parents think they could come after Labor Day." Poppy glanced at her own father, who was watching the morning unfold from his chair. He slowly raised his fork to his mouth, each bite taking concentrated effort. She would never get to have her father walk her down the aisle. She and Harrison had robbed him of that opportunity, and it made her want to cry.

Lily ran a finger across the page, looking at her notes. "No, that one is still open." She pulled a purple pen from the small fabric pencil case hooked into the binder and wrote something on her calendar. "Got you down."

Daisy sighed, "Oh, that's so exciting!" Then she looked at Poppy, "At least I'll get invited to one wedding." Poppy's heart sank at the barb. She deserved that one.

Hawthorne chimed in, "Who said you're invited?" which got a round of laughs as Daisy stuck her tongue out at him.

Harrison laughed with the group. What must he be thinking? This couldn't be any more different from his own family, with stilted conversation and fancy catering, as opposed to her mom's simple scrambled eggs and toast. But this was home.

Lavender had been quiet during the whole meal, and Poppy knew she needed to spend some time with her younger sister. Andi was the only one who knew the whole story. And hopefully, it would stay that way. Lavender and Daisy had known longer than the others that there was something with Harrison. Neither had any clue about the wedding, though, and were bound to be hurt. They were the sisters she was closest to, and on any other topic, the most likely to confide in. But she hadn't wanted to distract Daisy from her own project, or for Daisy to spill her secret. And she hadn't wanted to seem crazy to Lavender, who was always so calm and collected.

Daisy was the loud, fun one. Lavender was friendly but shy, more comfortable behind a computer. Rose was more like Daisy, comfortable in her own skin and more than willing to make a splash. Lily was calm and professional. Andi was a force to be reckoned with. Poppy never felt like she was anything but average. She wasn't loud. She wasn't shy. She wasn't friendly or confident. She was just...Poppy.

Yet, somehow, Harrison had chosen her. It didn't make sense as much as she tried to reason her way through it. Still, in the last few months it became increasingly obvious that her infatuation for Harrison hadn't died in high school. In fact, it had only grown stronger. Was she setting herself up for a lifetime of disappointed and unrequited love? Or could Harrison fall in love with her, for real? Not for some political ads.

It didn't make sense for Poppy to continue living on the farm, now that her family knew about the marriage. Which meant, it was time for Poppy to move in with Harrison. His little house in Terre Haute would now be *their* little house in Terre Haute.

After brunch, Poppy packed up her room with Lavender and Rose's help.

"I still can't believe you are married," Rose said as she pulled Poppy's clothes from the dresser and packed them in a suitcase.

"Me either," Lavender agreed. "And you didn't say anything."

"I really am sorry," Poppy sat on the edge of her bed. "It just happened so quickly."

"I should have known, after I saw the two of you that day at the Harvest Festival."

"We had barely started seeing each other then," Poppy laughed.

"It was still obvious that you were in love." Lavender must be remembering with a skewed memory, because there had been nothing between them that day beyond Harrison badgering her about being his wife.

"Oh, whatever." Poppy protested, the heat rising in her cheeks.

"You were! You guys were so cute walking around holding hands."

"Ugh, give me a break." Rose said.

"What, no romantic streak for Rose?" Poppy asked with a laugh.

"No, men are pigs. No wait, that's an insult to my hogs. Men are worse."

"Whoa. What happened?"

"I don't want to talk about it," Rose replied with a shake of her head.

"Oh, come on, Rose." Poppy tried to convince her baby sister to confide in them.

"So you get to keep all your secrets, but I'm supposed to spill everything? Fat chance. You know what, Poppy? Pack your own stuff. Or bring your secret husband over to help." With that, Rose stormed out.

Poppy looked at Lavender, who calmly opened another drawer and put stacks of t-shirts into a box. "What's with her?"

"She's got a point, you know. You broke our trust, Poppy. There are consequences to that." Poppy's heart sank. Lavender was right, but it still sucked.

"Do you all hate me?" she asked with a quiet

voice as she twisted her wedding ring around her finger.

Gently, Lavender sat next to her on the bed. "We don't hate you. It's just... hard to think that our sister got married and didn't want us there."

"It isn't that I didn't want you there! Please don't think that, Lovey." Poppy grabbed her sister's hand, resorting to begging.

Her sister flashed a small smile and Poppy felt a smidgen of hope blossom in her chest. Perhaps the relationships would recover. She had to pray that they would. Her sisters meant everything to her. She reached around and gave Lavender a hug. When they parted, Lavender took her hand again and flipped it over. "Okay, now give me a better look at that rock." She whistled, "I knew the Coulters had money, but whoa." Lavender studied the large diamond and intricate setting closely before commenting, "Maybe I should do a blog post about engagement ring trends." Poppy laughed at the random musing, her spirit lightening further at the completely random but wonderfully normal comment from Lavender. Everything was a bit crazy right now, but some things never changed.

They finished packing up her room and Poppy drove the truck over to Harrison's house. Her house.

She grabbed a box from the truck and knocked on the door, awkwardly balancing the box on her hip. The door swung open, and Harrison quickly grabbed the box from her and let her inside.

"Hey, I didn't expect you quite so soon."

Poppy attempted a smile. "Not too much stuff, really. Mostly clothes." She left behind a lot, mostly high school papers and college textbooks. It seemed weird to take her sheets and bedding to move in with her husband, so she'd left them behind.

"Well, I've made some good progress. Come, and I'll show you." He set the box down in the living room and led her into the hallway, past the guest bathroom where she'd gotten dressed for the Christmas party. She looked through the open door to her right and saw a bed with clothes piled on it. What in the world?

Then Harrison walked through the door at the end of the hall. She followed him into a large room, with a king size bed and soaring ceilings. "I can't take your bedroom, Harrison," she protested.

"It's yours. You will be here way more than I will, anyway. I already cleared out my closet, so I'll unload the truck while you start unpacking things."

Without leaving room for further argument, he left her alone, and Poppy looked around the big space. The comforter on the bed was a masculine navy-blue and tan, and only a few pieces of art dotted the walls. As she studied the space, it became increasingly obvious that a bachelor lived here. No extra pillows on the bed, no personal photos.

It felt strangely intimate to be in Harrison's room. Her room, she corrected. She sat on the bed for a moment, then stood again. Harrison's bed. Her room. She walked over to the closet, peering into the large walk-in. Her clothes would barely fill a corner in the giant closet. It was bigger than her office in the pole-barn.

She peeked into the bathroom next, her eyes widening at the walk-in shower and large jacuzzi tub.

"It's never been used," Harrison said over her shoulder, startling her. Poppy laid a hand over her racing heart as he continued, "Sorry, wasn't trying to scare you." He gestured to the tub, "I've never used it. Maybe it will finally do some good."

He wanted her to use his bathtub? Poppy blushed at the thought and shook her head. "Are you sure? I can use the guest room."

"I'm sure. I want you to feel at home here. I know this is all still a little strange," Poppy choked on a laugh, "but I'm trying here. Okay?"

She nodded. "Okay. Thank you."

"Now start unpacking, and I'll order delivery for dinner later."

"I guess that's one benefit to living in the city."

"One of many, I assure you." Harrison winked and Poppy grinned. She could do this. Harrison was her friend. And now, her roommate. And technically, husband. No big deal.

19

Harrison finished unloading the truck began helping Poppy unpack boxes and suitcases.

Pulling stacks of t-shirts, he arranged them neatly on the shelves in the closet. Next to him, Poppy hung up dresses and blouses on the hangers she brought with her. He tried to think of something to say? What could he say to his wife as she moved in to a bedroom they wouldn't share?

Setting the empty box aside, he grabbed another and opened it up. "Where do you want your—" Harrison choked, the words caught in his throat. What he initially thought was the strap of a tank top was actually attached to a white and red patterned bra, now hanging from the tip of his finger. His gaze shot to Poppy, placing a blue dress on a hanger. When she glanced up at him, Harrison dropped the piece of lingerie and cleared his throat.

The blush blooming on Poppy's face was surprisingly adorable, and Harrison's own embarrassment was likely leaving a similar color on his. What else would be hidden in these boxes? Maybe it would be better if she unpacked herself. "I'll just go order the food," he said before ducking out of the room. Harrison might not be a saint, but he was still a man. The sight of a woman's underthings was not something he had grown accustomed to. Perhaps living with a woman—his wife—would be more difficult than he thought. Especially if it meant seeing her bras and the inevitable images his mind conjured up.

He pushed the thoughts out of his mind and focused on ordering the Chinese food for dinner. He couldn't bring himself to walk back into the bedroom, so he just ordered a little of everything, hoping Poppy wasn't too picky. Harrison paid the driver and unpacked the food in the kitchen, setting out plates and glasses of water before walking down the hallway. There was only so much time he could kill before facing Poppy again.

Harrison knocked on the door frame, hesitant to enter. Was all her underwear put away? Opening the door slowly, he poked his head in. Poppy walked out of the closet, zipped up a suitcase on the bed, and moved it to the floor. A stack of broken-down boxes sat under the window across the room. "Wow, is that everything?"

Poppy nodded. "Yep. I guess I'm all moved in." The casual way she stated it stuck out. She seemed very relaxed about the whole thing, but why couldn't he keep his palms from sweating?

They ate dinner in the kitchen, and Harrison turned on the evening news he had recorded from the night before. It was comfortable and not remotely romantic—exactly what Harrison needed to remind himself where things stood between them. Poppy had officially invaded his space, and he was rather eager to return to Indianapolis the following week. It was, at least for now, lingerie-free.

When he was getting ready for bed, Harrison went to the guest bathroom, only to remember he'd left everything in the master bathroom, including his toothbrush and toothpaste. Poppy had left the living room about a half hour prior. Should he risk waking her up?

With a glance at the light coming under the door, he knocked lightly. Poppy cracked the door and he saw her concerned look. "Harrison?" she asked, confused. Her hair was damp, her skin soft and glistening.

He smiled, trying to alleviate her fears. Just because they had moved in together, nothing had changed. They were friends, nothing more. Or so he kept trying to tell himself. "Sorry, I just left a few things in your bathroom. Do you mind if I grab them real quick?"

Poppy stepped aside, and he saw her own toothbrush in her hand. She followed him into the bathroom and set her toothbrush in her bag. He tried not to notice the way her pajama shorts fell against her thighs. He tried to ignore the way she stood on her red-painted tiptoes to get close to the mirror, combing her long, auburn hair.

Her tank top clung to her curves, revealing her strong arms and the tantalizing shoulders he remembered from the Christmas party. They were tanner now, the warm days and sunshine giving her skin a bronze glow he couldn't help but want to touch.

Harrison stood near the door, mesmerized by the simple routine. He needed to get out of here, but first he needed his things. He stepped forward, trying to walk in front of Poppy, just as she stepped forward to try to let him behind. They bumped together, her damp hair tickling his arms. Searching for space,

Harrison stepped back and tried to go behind her, but Poppy tried to step backwards to let him go in front of her. They both stopped again in an awkward dance. Oh, for heaven's sake. They would be here all night, and Harrison was already desperate for distance between them. He placed his hands on her warm shoulders and held her in place as he walked between her small frame and the bathroom vanity. The entire room smelled like the citrusy lemon soap he had come to associate with Poppy. Moisture clung to his skin, the air heavy with it from the shower she'd taken.

Harrison closed his eyes at the thought of Poppy in his shower and pulled open the vanity drawer with too much force, causing it to slam as the drawer reached the end of its track.

Poppy raised her eyebrows at him and he ducked his head, intent on finding his toothbrush and getting out. The small drawer seemed impossibly full, and he couldn't see his toothbrush anywhere. Couldn't she see what she was doing to him?

Poppy stepped close, brushing her leg against his. "Can I help you find anything?" she asked sweetly.

Poppy knew she was being scandalous. But was it really scandalous when you were married?

"Nope, I got it." Harrison opened the door under the sink and grabbed a small, black toiletry bag. She stepped back, frustrated. He was completely unaffected by her.

Here she was, fresh out of the shower and in nothing but boxer shorts and a tank top, her hair still wet. And Harrison couldn't care less. When he'd knocked on her door, part of her had hoped... Well, it clearly didn't matter what she had hoped might happen. This was a disaster. So much for seducing her husband.

It seemed like they had been inching closer to something real. When he helped her with her zipper on the Christmas dress, had she been the only one breathless and tortured? Apparently, because Harrison was practically sprinting out of the bathroom.

He held up the bag as he walked out, his back to her. "Thanks. Goodnight!"

And just like that, Poppy was once again alone. She sighed and finished combing her hair before pulling it into a simple French braid so she wouldn't wake up to a tangled mess for church.

Then, she flipped off the light and slipped under

the comforter. Harrison mentioned that the sheets were clean, but it didn't stop her from imagining that she could smell him on the pillow, and she swore with every rumple of the comforter a cloud of Harrison's cologne hit her. The bed was huge compared to her bed at home, clearly made for two people.

Poppy had practically thrown herself at him in his bathroom, clearly not thinking straight—perhaps the water had been too warm in the shower. And instead of responding or kissing her goodnight, Harrison had barely noticed and gone to brush his teeth and sleep in the guest room.

How long would they be married before it felt real? How many nights would she have to lay here and dream about her husband while he slept in another bed?

Earlier today she'd told her family she loved him and wanted to start a family with him. It was awfully hard to start a family when he practically screamed at the sight of a bra and fled when she so much as touched him with bare legs.

If they were going to be married, maybe it was time to stop pretending she just thought of him as a friend. What was the worst that could happen? He'd already committed to forever. She considered laying it all on the line, but the thought of being rejected by him, again, was too much to bear. Even if she was his wife, there was nothing that said he had to love her. No, she had to let him fall in love with her in his own time. She couldn't force it. Harrison was stubborn, and the more she tried to convince him of one thing, the more he would be determined to do the other.

Poppy would persevere. And when Harrison was ready to accept his role as her husband, she would be there willing to be his wife.

20

Poppy's long skirts and simple braids had given Harrison no indication that she slept in tank tops and lounged around the house in soft, off-the-shoulder t-shirts and leggings that left little to the imagination. After church on Sunday, where they'd held hands and put on happy smiles for the public, they'd retreated to the privacy of his house.

Now, he was back in Indianapolis, gearing up for the return of the Senate session. Harrison had never been so grateful for his tiny Indianapolis apartment. Many of the senators made the trip back to their home district almost every night, or chose to stay in hotels on the rare occasion they needed to. But Harrison had the money and enjoyed the city. Especially now that his own house in Terre Haute had been invaded by his own personal siren.

He had a committee meeting later today and main session tomorrow. Senators Hawkins and Daniels had asked him for an early morning breakfast and he still had major work to do to push forward the TEACH Act. He'd been preoccupied lately and it wasn't good for his productivity.

He met the senators at a small, local cafe known for their farm-fresh ingredients. "Good morning, gentlemen." They made small talk while waiting for the food and enjoying their coffee.

When the food arrived, Senator Daniels shifted gears. "I'll get right down to business. We want your support on The Farm Business Act. It's good for jobs and the state revenues."

Harrison started to shake his head, but Daniels continued, "I know you've framed yourself as a local farm boy done good, but we are talking serious business here. There are million-dollar investors wanting to pour money into our state. You can't say no to that, Harrison. They estimate five hundred new jobs."

And how many local farmers does that put out of work? He didn't vocalize the thought. Better to bite his tongue and learn more. "What's the bottom line?"

Hawkins talked through the fiscal impact of the

bill and Harrison nodded. It did sound promising. The corporate farms could produce corn at impressive yields, and corn was federally subsidized, which would bring in additional revenue. Poppy was up for a tough fight.

"I'm sorry boys, I can't vote against the small farmers."

"Oh yeah, I heard all about your *wife*." Hawkins said the word with a sneer and Harrison wanted to punch the portly senator in the mouth.

Daniels chimed in, "We are prepared to return the favor by ensuring your TEACH Act passes committee and has bi-partisan support in main session."

Harrison stopped, a bite of omelet halfway to his mouth. "You would vote for TEACH? But didn't you vote to cut funding for teacher salaries just last year?"

Hawkins shrugged. "Things change. Like, we hope, your stance on the handouts we are giving to farms who don't use their land to its full potential."

Harrison was taken aback at the position Hawkins had just spoken. He thought about Bloom's farm and the amazing things they did there. Poppy's orchards, fields, and greenhouse were just the beginning. She used every inch of ground, and she provided produce to local markets that would otherwise come from states away.

On the other hand, obtaining bi-partisan support on his education bill would be a huge feather in his cap. Perhaps big enough to send him to the governor's office. It was certainly an option to consider. Without Hawkins and Daniels, it would be a major fight to get the TEACH Act to pass. But this deal would mean turning his back on small farms and, most of all, Poppy.

"Well, that's a very interesting point to consider, senators. I'm afraid I will need some more time to consider my stance." There, that would buy him some time. And it was true. He needed to figure out how he could somehow work this all out. In the end, the governor's office was the goal. Wasn't that the most important thing?

The lure that his colleagues were dangling in front of him was interesting, to say the least. He was very tempted to say yes and guarantee the success of his education bill.

"Wonderful. It is up for a vote at the end of next week. Should be enough time for you to determine if you stand on the side of progress or in opposition to it," Hawkins said smugly.

Harrison clenched his jaw and nodded curtly. "I said I would let you know."

Hawkins rapped a knuckle on the table and stood, tugging his suit coat down. "We'll be in touch, Senator."

When they left, Harrison sipped his coffee, only to find it had gone from warm and pleasant to acrid and bitter—much like his morning.

Committee meetings dragged on, a monotony of discussion and, more often than not, grandstanding by the author of the legislation. Instead of listening and participating, Harrison couldn't think of anything except the offer from Hawkins and Daniels. He'd been working on the TEACH Act for months, laying the groundwork and finalizing the language he wanted in the policy. It was going to be the cornerstone of his campaign, especially if it passed.

And for them to support the bill would make it that much more impressive. Of course, it would mean voting for the Farm Business Act. Which he didn't technically agree with. But what was the big deal about small farms paying less in taxes? That didn't really sound fair either.

Of course, the way Poppy talked, it would do more than just be a small burden. She talked as though it would literally put them out of business.

Harrison didn't know much about the business of Bloom's Farm, and his own family only had a livestock operation, which wasn't in the same boat.

He couldn't justify turning his back on Poppy and the deal he'd made. Even without the deal with Poppy, would he trade votes like a jaded politician? The thought made him cringe. What about those promises he made to God all those years ago?

Thankfully, he had a week or two to decide. Later this week, Poppy was coming for a date, where they would be photographed having a nice, intimate dinner at a local Indianapolis restaurant. Next week, they were scheduled to attend a fundraising dinner for Kid's Wish Charity. Harrison had always supported their cause, and Neil had insisted Poppy attend this year. He had paced and ranted about press exposure and connecting with donors until Harrison had finally relented.

It seemed like ages since the story broke in the papers, but it was only five days ago. Still, the news cycle moved quickly and it was already old news. The congratulatory handshakes he had received this morning from colleagues were casual and kind. No one suspected a thing.

"I move to adjourn for the day," came a voice to his left.

"Second," he said, jumping at the chance to wrap this up. After being in close quarters with Poppy all weekend at his house, he was looking forward to his sparse Indianapolis apartment.

Yet, as he lay in the silence of the empty apartment, he couldn't help but miss the vibrating awareness of knowing Poppy lay on the other side of the wall, in his bed. He couldn't help but wish to hear her brushing her teeth or humming a song as she grabbed a bedtime snack, like she had the night before.

Oh boy, he had it bad. But Harrison knew better than anyone that trying to make his marriage with Poppy into something more was a bad idea. Even now, he was considering turning his back on his promise to Poppy and pursuing his own interests. He knew, to some degree, that Poppy thought they would someday live like married couples should. But Harrison knew people didn't really love the real him. His parents had never been satisfied with plain old Harrison, focused entirely on what people saw. When he'd opened up to Stacy about his fears and failures, she'd turned around and fabricated an interview that had landed her the role as a morning news anchor. In politics, he couldn't afford to show people anything other than the polished, confident lawyer they expected. People loved Harrison Coulter, Senator and lawyer. They didn't love Harrison Coulter, workaholic and full of self-doubt.

No, if Poppy really knew him, she'd run away from this marriage faster than Easton trying to get back to the water. Harrison had to keep her at arm's length, because if she saw the real Harrison Coulter, she would never choose to stay. One thing about politics that hadn't been hard for Harrison was putting on a front. In most ways, he felt like he'd been doing that his entire life—trying to live up to the Coulter family name. His father could say what he wanted about Easton, but Harrison understood the pressure his brother felt. Whether self-imposed or outright expressed, being a Coulter meant certain things, and if you didn't live up to the standards? It was enough to make you feel trapped.

Poppy's family was kind and welcoming. They'd accepted Poppy's apology and immediately forgiven her for hurting them. She had been open and honest with him about her fears from the beginning, admitting her hesitation to dive into a marriage with him. Harrison had put on a brave face and focused on the goal. Right now, focusing on the goal could mean voting for the Farm Business Act and hurting Poppy. Harrison was already pretty well convinced he could only have one: love or success. And love was a long-shot by his calculations.

Still, maybe Poppy was different. She'd known him for nearly two decades. She knew all about his political aspirations, and she knew him when he was just an awkward teenager with braces. Did Harrison really have a chance at love with Poppy? Was that why God had led him to ask her to marry him? Maybe he was so stubborn that the only way he would admit to the possibility was if he were already committed for life.

21

The following week, Poppy drove to Indianapolis in the outrageously expensive SUV left in the driveway by Harrison. Apparently, the man thought he could control even more of her life. She was kind of surprised he hadn't sent her instructions about what to wear for their first official "date" as a married couple.

She pulled into the parking garage close to Harrison's apartment and walked around the block, carrying her small overnight bag. She'd be leaving late, after the date. But appearances were everything, as Harrison kept reminding her. Poppy smiled at the doorman as he greeted her, "Good afternoon, Mrs. Coulter."

Mrs. Coulter? That would take some getting used to.

Harrison pulled open the door, a finger over his lips. He pointed to his phone and mouthed, "Sorry," before turning away and speaking into the phone. "I understand what you are saying, Matthew, but I just don't agree." His voice faded as he turned the corner of the hallway and Poppy wandered in, closing the door behind her.

While Harrison's house in Terre Haute was cozy and humble, this apartment was sleek and modern. The floors were tiled and the soaring windows overlooked a maze of streets and gray buildings. The couches were black leather and low to the ground. A giant television dominated one wall. While large and impressive, the condo was ostentatious and cold.

Poppy hated every shiny, stainless-steel inch of this place.

Who wanted to live like this? Where was the green? At least Harrison's tiny house had a square of grass in the front and a tree in the back. This was like living in a cage with a kitchen.

Harrison came back through the hallway, ending his call. "Hey, glad you made it." He walked over to her in dress slacks and a button-down shirt with the sleeves rolled up and kissed her gently on the cheek. "How was the drive?"

"It was fine." She held up the car keys, "You really didn't have to buy me a car."

"And let you drive that bucket of rust all the way to the city? No way. Besides, we are married now. What's mine is yours." Poppy raised her eyebrows in surprise. That wasn't exactly a conversation they'd had yet. She knew Harrison had money, though she had no idea how much. Was it enough to buy a brand-new SUV straight up? Or had he taken a loan? Which would mean, had *they* taken a loan? This marriage thing was complicated.

Harrison held out his arms and looked around at the apartment, "Well, what do you think?" Poppy bit her lip and twisted her wedding ring around her finger. Should she tell him? Then, Harrison laughed. "It's okay. I'm sure you hate it."

"How'd you know?"

"You're Poppy Bloom. You love flowers and organic cotton sheets and essential oils. This place is one-hundred percent city living."

She looked around again and cringed. "It's like a mausoleum in here."

"Mausoleums don't have windows," Harrison countered.

"Windows that only look into other windows don't count," she said dryly.

"It's fine, I didn't expect you to like it. Tonight, we are going somewhere I really think you'll enjoy though."

Poppy's interest was piqued, and she quickly freshened up so they could leave.

They had dinner at a lovely farm-to-table restaurant nestled on the outskirts of Indianapolis, between the city and the suburbs. The dining room was intimate, with candlelit, rough-hewn tables and fresh flowers in mason jars. It was exactly the kind of place Poppy loved to eat.

After dinner, the chef came and greeted them. "Senator and Mrs. Coulter, thank you for joining us this evening." Poppy glanced up at the chef, preparing to put on her own version of a campaign smile.

Harrison laughed. "You can knock it off with the senator stuff, Pete. Pete, this is Poppy. Poppy, my college roommate, Pete Macintosh."

Poppy glanced at her husband. "Roommates?"

Pete smiled warmly, "Yep. Well, before I changed my major from Pre-law to Food Science and Health."

Poppy couldn't help but smile back at the strong

man in a crisp, white chef coat. He shook her hand, "Rumor has it you are a farmer?"

"I am. My family and I own an organic produce farm near Terre Haute."

"Now we are talking. What do you grow?" Immediately at ease, Poppy ran through the list of fruits and vegetables she grew, mentioning her intention to plant heirloom tomatoes this year. Pete clutched his heart, "Run away with me," he said with a twinkle in his eye.

With a laugh of surprise, Poppy looked at Harrison and back at Pete. She tipped her head back toward her husband. "What will we do with him?"

Pete leaned in conspiratorially. "Think anyone would miss him if he disappeared?"

Harrison narrowed his eyes, "Are you done plotting my demise with my wife, Petey?"

"Not quite," Pete said and then turned back to Poppy. "How did you end up with Mr. Indiana here, anyway?"

Well, now if that wasn't the million-dollar question. "We've been friends since high school," Poppy said simply.

Pete clucked his tongue and shook his head. "Can't compete with history." He flashed a smile and laid a hand on Harrison's shoulder. "Congratulations, dude. Looks like you married way up."

Harrison smiled tightly, "Thanks, Pete. Dinner was excellent, as usual."

Harrison wasn't his usual charming self. Did her joking with Pete really bother him, or was there something else going on? Still, the food had been amazing and she gave her compliments to Pete. "Sometime you'll have to come visit the farm. We are still working on supplying restaurants in addition to our farmers markets and CSA baskets."

"I'd love that. I wish I could be even closer to the ingredients, you know?"

Poppy understood. There was something about creating a menu based on what you knew, first-hand, was fresh and ready to harvest. Maybe if they ever opened a restaurant at Bloom's Farm, the chef would be able to do that.

After dinner, Harrison had arranged an evening tour of the capital building. As they wandered through the soaring four-story atrium, their footsteps echoed on the white marble tile. Poppy looked at the sculptures and soaring columns, amazed that her husband came to work in this building. Brass chandeliers gave the space a sense of history, along with the artwork and the balconies overlooking the main hallways. Harrison rattled off facts about the statehouse as Poppy listened.

During a break in his spiel, Poppy commented, "It must be surreal to work here."

"Sometimes I walk through the rotunda and wave to the governor, and I think how crazy it is."

Poppy ducked her head. "I can't imagine what it would be like to have everyone know who you are... Sometimes I feel like I'm just an afterthought in our family." She fidgeted with her ring and then met his surprised gaze.

"You can't mean that? Your family adores you, Poppy." His brown eyes studied her intently, confusion written on his face.

"Sure, they love me. But sometimes I'm not sure they really know me."

Harrison scoffed, "You say that like just because people know my name, they know the real me. The truth is, almost no one I work with knows the real me. Not like you do." He stepped close and Poppy's heart raced. Harrison brushed her cheek with the back of his fingers and Poppy's eyes fell closed.

Harrison studied Poppy's perfect, heart-shaped face. The capital building was quiet, closed to the public by now. Other than a few security guards he recognized, there was no one here to put on a show for. If he kissed Poppy now, it wouldn't be for a photo op or to convince his college roommate that their relationship was real. It would be only because he wanted to kiss her. Which he did, desperately, if he was being honest with himself. The urge to lower his mouth to hers and claim those lips was nearly overwhelming.

His fingers traced down Poppy's cheek and behind her ear, down her neck. Poppy's mouth fell open slightly as she drew in a sharp breath at the contact, and Harrison's mind went blank. All the reasons why he should step away were suddenly gone. As was the guilt about the vote he might make next week. There was nothing except Poppy's skin against his and then, the feel of her lips under his, as he stepped close and gave in to the desire he'd been fighting for weeks.

Poppy's lips yielded under his, soft and warm and impossibly sweet. He turned his fingers and tucked his hand around to the nape of her neck, pulling her closer, tendrils of her hair brushing his skin, and the wave of lemon enveloping him. Intoxicating him. Her body pressed into him and he wrapped his other arm around her waist, spreading his palm and pulling her up, desperate to have her closer.

Filling his senses with Poppy meant a blessed silencing of the doubts and fears and guilt of the decisions ahead for him. Right now, there was nothing beyond the two of them in the quiet rotunda of the state house.

Reluctantly, Harrison broke the kiss but continued holding Poppy close, unwilling to let her go and shatter the moment completely. Poppy's eyes opened and she met his gaze, her warm brown eyes dark and inviting, tempting him to kiss them closed again.

Instead, he cleared his throat. "Poppy, I know getting married to me was the last thing you thought would happen when I called you last year. But I hope you don't regret it."

Poppy's half-dazed smile filled him with satisfaction. She shook her head slightly, "No, I don't regret it."

He bent down and kissed her lightly again. All the reasons he needed to keep his distance and not fall for Poppy, every objection, seemed weak and distant. She fit too perfectly in his arms, looked at him with too much adoration and respect. Especially here, in these austere halls. It would be too easy to get used to, to rely on her as a cornerstone of his life.

"Should we continue the tour?" he asked quietly, stepping away but taking her hand in his.

He saw the questions die on her lips before she nodded. "Where is your office?" she asked, curiously.

Harrison smiled and led her up the stairs through a maze of hallways. "It's not nearly as glamorous as the rest of the building, especially when the doors to the Senate Chamber are locked." He unlocked the door and let her in the office, then walked across the small room to the windows and another door. "Our offices overlook the chambers. Come here," he said, standing next to a large window. Looking down, they could see the uniform wooden desks and blue chairs, one for each senator.

"Where do you sit?"

Harrison pointed to his seat, in the second row just to the left of center. He did love this view. He loved the wood and the blue carpet, the pomp and formality. History was made in these halls. Would he make history with his education bill? Or would it die in committee along with his chance to be governor?

22

Harrison came home Thursday night since the debate dragged on ahead of the scheduled recess. The session would reconvene next week which would mean a three-day weekend, but he really needed to catch up with things at the law firm.

If he waited until the morning, it would only mean a barrage of meetings and appointments, with no time to actually respond to emails or read the depositions. Instead, Harrison went to the office after getting back into town. He ordered takeout for dinner as he tackled a proposed settlement agreement and responded to emails he'd received since last week. It was after midnight when Harrison parked in front of the garage of his familiar gray bungalow, a yawn escaping from his lips.

Fiona wound a figure-eight between his legs as he came in, and he gave her an affectionate pat before closing the door, shrugging out of his coat and tossing it on the arm of the sofa in the dark. Then he ambled down the hallway to the master bedroom while slipping off his dress slacks and shirt. In the darkness, he tossed them in the general direction of the closet and crawled into bed, falling immediately into a blissful sleep.

THERE WAS a man in her bed. The thought had Poppy's eyes flying open before it was even complete. It was still dark in her room, but it was no longer silent. Soft, rhythmic snoring came from the other side of the giant king-sized bed she now called her own. She propped herself up on her elbows to look, her mouth going dry at the sight of broad, muscled shoulders as Harrison laid on his stomach, face turned away from her.

"Harrison!" she whispered.

There was no response, except another snore.

"Harrison, wake up!" she tried again, pushing against the firm arm strewn across the pillow. It didn't budge.

Should she get a cup of water? What was the protocol here? Finally, Poppy tried to shove Harrison away from her side of the bed where he was encroaching on her space. Not that there wasn't plenty, but it was the principal of the thing. What was he doing here?

"Harrison James Coulter!" Finally, he stirred.

"Hmmm?"

"You are in my bed!" she stage-whispered.

"I second the motion; no more bananas," Harrison's nonsensical ramblings faded into mumbling.

What on earth? Now he was talking in his sleep, just great.

Poppy fell back on her pillow and looked up at the vaulted ceiling. Harrison was lying in bed next to her with no shirt on. Hadn't she had this dream before?

Poppy hesitantly laid her hands on his side and back, just below his shoulder. His skin was warm and smooth under her fingers. Not letting her thoughts linger there, she gave one last effort to rouse him with a shove.

Harrison rolled over onto his side and the arm that had been up by his head was suddenly wrapped around Poppy's waist as he tucked her close to him. He gave a contented sigh, "Mmm, lemon."

Poppy's heart flip-flopped, and she turned onto her side, letting herself enjoy the warmth of her husband. At least he wasn't snoring anymore. She'd worry about the rest in the morning.

Used to rising before the sun, Poppy woke up early. Harrison's breathing was still steady and deep, and his arm rested heavy across her midsection. She tried to slip under it and out of the bed, but his arm tightened, holding her in place. Poppy relaxed back into the comfortable cocoon of the blankets and the solid warmth of his body, turning slightly so she could watch his face.

"It's not even morning," Harrison groaned

"It's five AM," Poppy responded.

Then he opened one eye, as though surprised to hear her voice. "Poppy?" he asked, confusion and sleepiness written all over his face.

She raised an eyebrow, "Were you expecting someone else?"

Harrison leaned up, glancing around the room. Poppy immediately missed him, but took the opportunity to scoot away from him and sit at the edge of the bed. "This is my room," he said, confused.

Not exactly a quick one on the uptake early in the morning. "Your *old* room."

"Right, my old room." He looked at Poppy, then down at the bed. "I crawled in bed with you last night?"

Poppy nodded. "And you were quite stubborn in your refusal to leave it."

Harrison smiled a crooked grin and sat up. "Sorry about that. I'm a pretty heavy sleeper."

With the sheet around his waist, there was nothing Poppy wanted more than to crawl back under the covers and see what Harrison's heartbeat sounded like. Instead, she sat up and grabbed a cotton robe to cover her bare shoulders.

"Late night?" she asked.

Harrison rubbed his eyes with his fingers. "Yeah. Got in late from Indianapolis and then stopped by the office to try to get a head start on my weekend workload." Harrison's bare feet appeared at the edge of the bed, and Poppy walked out of the room toward the kitchen and the high-end coffee maker she'd fallen in love with. She did not need to see if Harrison slept in shorts or boxers. Her face flushed at the possibilities. Had she really just slept for several hours tucked against him?

Determined to pretend it was not a big deal, Poppy started the coffee and pulled out the organic kale and strawberries she had brought from her stock of frozen produce at the farm. It would be a good day for a green smoothie.

Harrison ambled in, still shirtless but donning a pair of gray sweat pants that hung just low enough on his waist to make her mouth go dry. Poppy was going to turn into a pile of ash if Harrison didn't start wearing clothes around the house.

She cleared her throat, "Coffee?"

"Thanks."

She poured him a mug and then one for herself. Then she eyeballed the ingredients for her smoothie into the small blender. "Smoothie?"

Harrison sipped his coffee, wincing at the temperature and then glanced at her. "What kind?"

"Kale and strawberry."

He grimaced, "I'll pass."

"Suit yourself. Kale is a superfood, loaded with antioxidants and vitamins." Talking about vegetables was safer than talking about what happened last night.

"It tastes like freshly mowed grass smells. The cows at the farm—"

Poppy turned to hide her smile and pulsed her blender, drowning out Harrison's objections to her choice of vegetables.

Her smoothie complete, Poppy carried it over to the table along with her coffee. The sun was just starting to peek over the horizon. Harrison stood and leaned his hip on the counter, one ankle crossed over the other. "About last night—" he started.

"It's fine," Poppy interrupted. "It was obviously a mistake and you were very tired. No harm, no foul."

Harrison rubbed his jaw, "Well, yes. It was a mistake but—"

Poppy stood quickly, "I totally understand. It didn't mean anything." Then, she dumped the last of her now lukewarm coffee into the sink and grabbed the smoothie. "I'm going to go take a shower and get dressed. I'll see you tonight, I guess?"

Harrison frowned but nodded. "Yep. Tonight."

Poppy scurried down the hall and into the refuge of the master bedroom, her gaze falling briefly on the tangled sheets of the king-sized bed. Her eyes stung from tears she couldn't let fall. Harrison had climbed into bed with her and wrapped his arms around her all night. But it didn't mean anything.

~

Harrison watched his wife make her escape from the kitchen and then stared into the dark brown coffee she had made for him. Waking up next to Poppy had been a surprise. He vaguely remembered coming home and walking through the pitch-black house, walking down the hallway and—yep. There it was.

Still, he wouldn't have expected to wake up, holding Poppy to his side like some cuddly couple. He definitely hadn't expected how strong the urge was not to let her go. She'd said it was a mistake, which was true. But she'd also said it didn't mean anything. But that wasn't necessarily true.

Something had become crystal clear to him in the dark fog of the morning. Harrison's life, and even his house and his bed, were better with Poppy in it. And he planned to tell her exactly that when she ventured back out of the bedroom.

An hour later, she finally emerged, her damp hair braided and wearing one of the loose, colorful skirts he'd come to associate with her. A quilted purse with a long strap was slung across her body, and she wore a sturdy cream-colored button-down shirt. Poppy looked every bit the organic produce farmer as she slipped on her cowboy boots.

He watched her silently, suddenly unsure of his words. He, Harrison Coulter, who always had an answer ready for a waiting reporter or debating senator, didn't know what to say. How could he suddenly tell her that his feelings were growing real and far stronger than he'd thought possible? Would she think it was just because they'd slept together, in the literal sense of the word?

Maybe tonight, when they had another evening alone together he could bring it up. Poppy was special. She deserved more than a five-minute conversation on her way out the door.

"See you later," Poppy said as she ducked out the door.

Reluctantly, Harrison got ready to go to the office, already dreading the pile of calls he needed to make. He pulled into his reserved parking space and locked his car after grabbing his briefcase.

"Good morning, Senator," the receptionist greeted him. She didn't look familiar. They seemed to go through an endless parade of temps around here. He nodded his acknowledgment and then passed through the doors in the clear glass walls to the offices that lay beyond. His personal assistant and paralegal waited just around the corner.

"Good morning, Senator," Janet parroted the chirpy voice of the receptionist.

He gave her a sidelong glance as she burst into laughter and handed him a manila folder. "Good morning, Janet."

Whereas Bethany was old enough to be his mother and had been around the capital far longer than Harrison, Janet and Harrison had joined the firm the same summer, him after graduation and her as a paralegal intern. As he had risen in the ranks, he'd brought Janet along with him. They had struck up an unlikely friendship; the privileged golden-boy and the rough-around-the-edges graduate of the School of Hard Knocks.

There had been rumors about the two of them for years, but Janet only laughed when someone brought it up, mocking his most-eligible-bachelor nomination and plastering copies of the magazine all over the women's restrooms at the firm. It had earned her a written warning from the other partners, but copies had also found their way into his files and meeting agendas for the next month as all the paralegals joined in on the fun.

Janet fawned over him with fake adoration. "Oh,

please, Senator. Notice me, notice me!" She laughed again, "Girl must not have heard the whole happily married news report." Janet tapped her lips with a sparkly fingernail, "I think she might have been on spring break. Yep, I remember. Spring break in Florida."

They walked into Harrison's office and he sat down. "Are you done?"

"What? You've barely been here for two weeks. I've got a lot of time to make up for."

"Feel free to not. I need to leave by five today."

Janet raised her eyebrows in surprise. "You feel okay, boss?"

"Let's just get to work so we can leave."

"No objections here. I just usually plan on staying until at least nine or ten when you are here. Wait a second, does that mean I won't get Dragon Palace delivery covered by the firm tonight?"

Harrison rolled his eyes at his friend, "I'll buy your dinner myself if you can make sure I am out of here by five. Deal?"

By way of a response, Janet shifted into business mode. "You've got the partner's meeting at 9:30. Before that, I think you can squeeze in," she pulled four pink call slips, "these calls. Whichever you don't get to, I'll call while you are upstairs."

Say what you wanted about Janet's larger-than-life personality, she was an excellent worker and had a nearly perfect memory that made her an outstanding paralegal.

Harrison grabbed the pink call slips and picked up his phone, shooing Janet from his office, already looking forward to the time when he could return home to his wife.

23

Poppy drove home, irritated with her new living situation. It would be far easier to clean up if she were still living at home. But no, here she was, covered in mud and too stubborn to ask one of her sisters for a change of clothes. It would be admitting that she couldn't take care of the farm and be married to Harrison.

Stupid compost tumbler. The bottom had fallen off when she was trying to tighten the screws. Which meant she was covered in scraps of food and hay and dirt. It had been warm today too, so the mixture was especially fragrant.

Poppy parked her gray farm truck on the street, having refused to take the SUV to the farm, and made her way inside the house, eager to shed her no-longer-cream-colored shirt and maybe try out that giant soaking tub of Harrison's.

Once inside, Poppy stopped her in her tracks. Soft music played; it was one of her favorite Christian singers. Harrison was in the kitchen, in jeans and a casual button-down shirt, stirring something at the stove. Harrison could cook? And even more surprising, Harrison was already home?

She glanced at the table, set with dishes and candles lit. A salad was already waiting on the plate.

"Um, hi?"

At her voice, Harrison spun around, spoon in hand. "Welcome home, Mrs. Coulter." He moved toward her and Poppy stepped back, gesturing at the state of her outfit.

"Sorry, attack of the compost. It's been a bit of a rough day."

Harrison smiled, "Okay. This won't be ready for about twenty more minutes. Want to grab a shower and then come back out?"

He handed her a glass of wine and turned back to the stove. Poppy felt a bit like she had entered the Twilight Zone. Hadn't Harrison warned her that he worked late on the few days he was in the office during the senate session? That he worked weekends to keep up with both jobs?

Yet, it was barely six o'clock and he was home. Cooking her dinner. Was there a more attractive sight in the world?

Still processing, Poppy carried her wine back to the bedroom and ignored the unmade bed as she entered the bathroom and turned on the shower. There was a handy shelf built into the wall that made for a perfect place to set her wine.

After her shower, Poppy considered changing into her normal comfy leggings. But the picture of a candlelit table had her reaching for a floral sundress instead. Whatever had gotten into Harrison, she was going to enjoy being doted on.

She reapplied makeup and braided her hair, leaving the bottom half down and studying the final effects in the foggy mirror. Her dark coloring came from her father, only Hawthorne, Poppy and Rose had inherited his dark hair and eyes. Everyone else wore the golden tresses of their mother. Once, in an ill-conceived plan to get Harrison's attention, she'd attempted to bleach her dark curls at home with Daisy's help. The golden-orange tone had been horrendous, and her hair had been a dry, tangled mess for nearly a year.

Harrison had given it one look during the

Student Council meeting and completely ignored it. "Can you lead up the Prom committee?"

Poppy fingered the strands of hair she'd left framing her face. So many years wasted pining after Harrison Coulter, or angry with him for not seeing what he'd done to her. And here she was, in the house they shared and about to join him for a romantic dinner.

What was God trying to do to her?

She swallowed the last bit of the wine and straightened her shoulders.

Harrison grinned at Poppy when she entered the dining room. She looked beautiful, her hair in a playful braid and her empty wineglass in hand. He stepped away from the plates he was filling and pulled her in for a hug. "Hi."

She smiled up at him. "Hi."

He buried his face in her hair, "Mmmm. Lemon."

Poppy giggled and tried to pull away. "You said that last night, you know."

"What? When?"

"In your sleep. Or half-sleep."

That was interesting, but not all that surprising. He was pretty sure the scent of lemon would forever be associated with kissing Poppy. "Hmm, well, it does smell better than the compost you were wearing earlier. More wine?" he released her and grabbed the bottle of wine, refilling the glass she held up for him.

"So, care to tell me what all of this is about?" she gestured to the table and the wine.

"Can't I just surprise my beautiful wife with a romantic dinner for two?"

"Not really, unless you want your beautiful wife to be completely confused about your intentions."

"Is that what I've done? Have I confused you, Poppy?" he fingered a strand of auburn hair near her jawline. Poppy swallowed and then nodded. "I'm sure it's not nearly as completely as you have confused me, my love."

Her eyes flew open and Harrison met her gaze, full of questions.

"I can honestly say, I didn't expect this. Poppy, I thought I could be married to you, and that maybe years down the road it would turn into a romantic love. We were friends for years and I never wanted anything more. But since we've been married? I'm completely taken with you, Poppy Bloom Coulter. The very thought that you are my wife forever makes my every moment brighter. I know you might not be there quite yet, and that's okay. I just wanted you to know where my heart is. And maybe ask if you'd be willing to let me 'date' you and see where this goes." Harrison held his breath, watching her face for any clue about how she felt. Moments between them flashed, memories of times when Harrison was completely overwhelmed by Poppy's presence and she seemed completely unaffected by him. What would she say now that she knew how he felt?

Poppy stepped away and he dropped his hand. She took a drink of her wine and set it carefully on the counter, her back to him. "I loved you."

Loved? As in, past tense? "Come again?"

"In high school. I loved you desperately, despite insisting to everyone else that we were just friends. We were the exception to the rule that said guys and girls couldn't just be friends. Except we weren't. Because I wanted more. When neither of us had a date to prom, I was secretly thrilled we would get the chance to make good on the agreement we'd made as freshmen. But then you took Melanie." Poppy turned back to look at him, tears in her eyes. "You didn't choose me then, Harrison."

The hurt in her eyes made him wish he could turn back time. How had he not known about her feelings for him? Was he so oblivious? "I'm choosing you now, Poppy."

She twisted her wedding ring. "Are you? Or are you stuck with me?"

Harrison crossed the space between them in two steps, taking her in his arms. "Poppy, I am choosing you. I would choose you a hundred times over. I couldn't see what God was doing when he told me you were the one for this crazy plan of mine, but now I do. I love you, Poppy. And I'm going to spend the rest of my life proving it to you."

Then, he pressed his lips against hers, tasting the sweet red wine and winding his hand into the hair at the nape of her neck. What he couldn't say in words —the apologies and the reassurances—he would convey like this. Poppy leaned into him and he deepened the kiss, brushing her upper arms with his hands. He tasted the tears and she shuddered in his arms. Harrison broke the kiss and leaned his forehead against hers, leaving her nowhere to look but at him.

"What's wrong, beautiful?"

She sniffed. "I love you, Coulter."

Harrison's heart lifted at her words. "Really?" he asked, because he needed to be sure. He'd handed Stacy his heart and she'd ripped it out. Poppy would never be so careless, but his deeply hidden insecurities needed reassurance.

"Really. I'm not sure I ever really stopped."

That was one way to make him feel both incredible and foolish. It was time to lighten the mood, though. "Tell me the truth, Poppy. Did you vote for me?"

She smiled at his question,"I'll never tell."

Harrison tucked her against his chest and laid his chin on top of her head. "I'm so sorry I hurt you."

"It's okay. You were a dumb high school boy."

"Yes, I definitely was. Melanie Crocker turned out to be a terrible kisser." Poppy laughed and smacked his shoulder.

"You're awful."

"Maybe," Harrison said, "but you love me." Nothing could dampen his spirits tonight. They ate the dinner he had cooked and turned on a basketball game while Poppy curled up beside him on the couch. He slept in the guest room, but for the first time, he really thought their future might look more like a traditional love match than an arranged marriage. Still, they had a long way to go before they were ready to cross those lines. Even if he would wake up wishing he held her like he had this morning.

24

Reginald Coulter always said cows were better than horses. There was more money in beef than in races. Still, Harrison wasn't sure you could beat the view of the Indiana countryside from the top of a horse.

He and Poppy had arrived at the farm for Saturday morning brunch, apparently it was a weekly thing and mandatory for all Bloom children. Of which he now counted. "Don't even try to get out of it by claiming you have to work," Poppy warned him. "Mom is an expert at laying on the guilt in a way that makes you promise to do better without even realizing she orchestrated it."

"Maybe my mom needs lessons. She lays the

guilt on hard, but it doesn't seem to have much effect."

After brunch, Poppy asked if he wanted to ride. It had been years, but he still remembered how. The gentle rolling hills of Bloom's farm were starting to turn from brown to green, making him realize that spring was here. Poppy gave him a tour of the pastures and her fields, then came to a small hill. He could see neat rows of wooden supports with vines growing on them.

"Is this new?" he asked.

"Welcome to the vineyard portion of Bloom's Farm and Vineyard." Now that she said it, he did remember that the sign above the main entrance had the full name on it. But he'd never thought much of it.

"Cool. You grow grapes here?"

Poppy nodded. "I planted them about five years ago. Right now, I make about two batches of wine each year, but I'm getting better and hope to expand it more. All the proceeds from the wine go to IOSFA's urban farming programs."

"Urban farming?"

"They help plant community gardens in the inner-city neighborhoods, where food deserts mean families don't have access to a grocery store with fresh produce."

Harrison nudged his horse closer until he could reach, and he laid his hand on Poppy's leg. "That's really amazing, Poppy."

She turned away from the vineyard and smiled at him. "It's not much, but it's a little something I can do."

Harrison studied the vineyard, spotting a group of white animals at the bottom of the valley. "Are those...sheep?" he asked.

Poppy smiled. "Yep. They keep the grass in the vineyard short and they don't eat the grapes. That was Rose's idea. Plus, we sell their wool to an artist in Indianapolis."

Poppy's hair rustled in the wind and she pulled it around her shoulder. She glanced at him and Harrison stared, amazed at the woman in front of him. Her deep, abiding love for the land and the causes that had grabbed her heart were nothing short of incredible.

"I love you," he said simply, unable to find words any more fitting for the overwhelm of admiration and awe he felt.

Color rose in her cheeks and she looked back at

her vineyard before meeting his eyes again. "I love you, too."

Technically, he needed to go to the office and continue digging his way out of the pile waiting for him. But instead, he asked, "Should we go home?" Poppy nodded in response and turned her horse back toward the stables. There was nothing that sounded better than an afternoon at home with her.

Harrison returned to Indianapolis feeling lighter than he had in weeks. Things with Poppy were in a really good place, and his education bill was up for discussion in committee. The TEACH Act would be how he set himself apart from the competition for the governor's seat next year. He still had to figure out how to navigate Hawkins and Daniels insistence on his support of the farm bill, though. The thought of voting for it had his stomach turning. Publically, it wouldn't be hard to justify. The mega farms would increase revenues and create jobs. At least on the surface.

But Harrison was from farm country. It would also be easy for his opponents to attack him for voting against his base. It felt like a lose-lose situation.

The farm bill was up for vote next Thursday. He had until then to figure it out. In the meantime, he would work on his own legislation and making sure it had as much support as possible before it came up for a vote, with or without Hawkins and Daniels on board.

"Senator Whitman," he called to the balding head of the Education and Career Development Committee, "Glad I caught you this morning!"

"Harrison, how are you? And how is that new wife of yours?" Whitman asked, wiggling his eyebrows suggestively.

"She's great, back in Terre Haute until Wednesday's fundraiser. I was hoping to talk with you a bit about the TEACHER Act. It's on the docket for your committee today, and I just wanted to see if you had any questions."

Whitman clicked his tongue and shook his head. "No, no questions, Coulter. It's a solid piece of policy." He leaned in and spoke quietly, "But you should know I've been told to stall it."

Harrison stumbled. He quickly caught himself and ushered Whitman over to the side of the large marble hallway. “What do you mean? Why would you stall it?”

Whitman yanked at his collar. He looked awfully clammy, but the sixty extra pounds he carried could have something to do with it. “Hawkins is adamant that we wait for the farm bill to pass before I let your bill out of committee.”

Harrison tipped his head back and groaned. “That's ludicrous. The two are entirely unrelated!”

Whitman frowned, “I'm sorry. I've got my own issues to worry about. I'll do my best, Harrison, but I'm up for reelection soon and I can't afford to alienate the party. You know how it is,” he offered with a less-than-comforting pat on Harrison's shoulder.

Yes, Harrison knew how it was. Unfortunately, with every week he spent in politics, he knew more about exactly how it was.

So, Hawkins and Daniels weren't just going to let him choose whether to vote for their bill. They were going to hold his own policy hostage. Not only would they not support his bill, they would actively campaign against it. He wasn't going to be able to get out of this unscathed. Either he voted for their bill and Poppy hated him. Or he voted against it and kissed his own bill goodbye, and likely—his chance at governor with it.

This was the crud he hated in politics. His feet were to the fire and there was nothing he could do about it.

A rock and a hard place. What was he supposed to do?

25

Two nights later, they had a fundraiser for the local Kids' Wishes Foundation. The event was held annually for their biggest donors, and Harrison had been donating for years. Unfortunately, so had Senator Hawkins.

Harrison danced with Poppy, holding her close and whispering to her how beautiful she looked. Hawkins tapped him on the shoulder. "Harrison, my boy. Mind if I cut in?"

"Actually, I think I'd prefer my wife stays by my side tonight," Harrison said sharply.

Poppy frowned at him and gave a gracious smile to Senator Hawkins. "Harrison, don't be rude. I'd be happy to dance with you, Senator."

"Wonderful!" And with that, Harrison was left

alone on the dance floor, praying that the conversation wouldn't venture into political territory. Hawkins was still convinced Harrison was going to vote his way.

And if Hawkins told Poppy? Well, Harrison would have some major explaining to do. It would hardly matter to Poppy if Harrison hadn't said yes. The truth was, he'd considered betraying her and that would be enough to land him in the doghouse. It was enough to make him wonder what she even saw in him.

Poppy laughed at something Hawkins said as Harrison watched, his eyes glued to the couple in the middle of the dance floor, searching for any sign of distress.

As she spun, Harrison saw Poppy's eyes searching for his. Her smile was gone, and then she disappeared behind another couple. He craned his neck to find her again, but her eyes were on the senator, and there was no laughter in them.

"I'm sorry, Senator. You must be mistaken. Harrison would never vote in favor of the Farm Business Act."

Hawkins laughed and the sound made Poppy's blood run cold. "That's what I thought, but Daniels insisted we ask him anyway. It was a stroke of genius to agree to back his TEACH Act in return. Nothing Harrison likes better than funding teacher salaries."

Poppy's mouth fell open. Harrison had traded votes? After everything they had agreed to? Even though he knew how much she loved the farm and what the Farm Business Act would do, he had traded his support in exchange for votes on his beloved education bill?

"Excuse me. I need to use the ladies' room."

"It's been a pleasure, Mrs. Coulter. I look forward to seeing you again. Perhaps you and Harrison could join myself and Marjorie for a double date. It'd be a nice show of bi-partisanship, don't you agree?"

Poppy couldn't bring herself to do anything but nod before she walked away, her vision blurry from the unshed tears. How could Harrison do this to her? What had been the point in his big declaration of love if in the end, he was just going to choose his career over her?

Why did she always come second? Lost in the shuffle at home, overlooked by Harrison in the past. Poppy was always destined to come second. She had thought this was finally her chance. For some unknown reason, Harrison had chosen her to be his wife. Had she even been his first choice? For all she knew, he had asked other women—smarter women, most likely, who had said no to his crazy proposal.

Not Poppy, though. Somehow, she was the foolish one who hoped he would actually fall in love with her, that her unrequited love would somehow have a chance if only he was stuck with her for life. This was a dumb idea.

Poppy stood in the washroom, staring at her reflection with red-rimmed eyes and blotchy skin. She didn't look like the polished politician's wife she was supposed to be. She'd much rather be at the farm, anyway. Hadn't she thought as much when they arrived at the swanky dinner?

Poppy dried her eyes, trying her best to remove the mascara streaks. She needed to talk with Harrison. Quickly, she texted him. **We need to talk. I'll be outside when you are ready to leave.**

Moments later, Harrison replied. **I'll get the car.**

A trio of well-dressed women entered the restroom and Poppy skirted them, keeping her face turned away so they might not recognize her. Her phone vibrated in her hand and she saw Harrison's next message come through. **Also... I'm sorry. Please let me explain.**

Oh, she would let him explain alright. Not that there was anything he could say. But he deserved at least that much. Maybe Senator Hawkins had misunderstood. Maybe Harrison hadn't agreed to vote the way Hawkins said. Poppy could only hope that was the case. Because if it turned out Harrison was going to vote for the Farm Business Act, this entire agreement to be his wife was null and void. Even if it would rip her heart out to give back the ring and leave his house. It would be infinitely better than being married to a liar and a manipulator.

Poppy ducked into the elevator and rapidly pressed the button until the doors blessedly began to close. A tanned arm holding a shiny silver clutch reached through the crack, forcing the doors to reopen.

Following the arm into the elevator was a bleach-blond nightmare in a skin-tight dress. Stacy. Poppy closed her eyes and tipped her head toward the ceiling. Was God serious right now?

"Oh, Paula! Congratulations on the wedding," Stacy said in her shrill, false-friendly tone.

"It's Poppy," she replied dryly.

"Of course, it is." Stacy waved away the correction. "Rough night, sweetie?"

Poppy nearly growled, but just shook her head.

"You must be realizing what I figured out last year. Harrison Coulter will always care more about his career than about a woman. It's hard to make a difference when he doesn't let you in."

Thankfully, the doors opened, and Stacy sauntered out. Poppy waited a beat and then followed, desperate to find Harrison and get out of here. Maybe Stacy was right. All Poppy had ever wanted was to make a difference. In some way, she thought being married to Harrison would give her some influence, a way to stand up for the things she believed in. But if she wasn't even worth keeping a promise to? What kind of impact could she really have?

Poppy exited the hotel to find Harrison already waiting inside his car. She climbed in and closed the door to shut out the world. The car was eerily quiet as Harrison looked at her.

"Poppy, I—"

"Let's go," she interrupted. She needed to stand up, walk around and look Harrison in the eyes while they had this conversation.

He didn't argue, and before long they had completed the short drive back to the apartment in silence. Once inside the cold, modern space, Poppy turned around to face her husband.

"Did you agree to vote in favor of the Farm Business Act?"

"Poppy, it's a bit more complicated—" Her anger surged and she stepped closer.

"Did you agree?"

"They are holding the TEACH Act hostage, stonewalling me in committee." At his words, Poppy's mouth fell open. Even though she'd been questioning all night whether it was true, something about hearing Harrison admit it himself hurt even worse. "In exchange for my vote, Hawkins would guarantee bi-partisan support for my bill. But Poppy, I hadn't decided yet!"

He stepped close, but Poppy turned away so he only brushed the side of her arm with his chest. She stared at Fiona, who wisely figured this was not the time to bother them and was watching from a safe distance away on the armchair.

"I have to look at the big picture, Poppy. Passing the education bill would be a huge victory on my path to the governor's office. It's just one little vote."

Poppy felt the familiar sting of tears, "It's not just one little vote, Harrison. It's my entire life! It's my family's farm. It's Andrew Treat's farm and his family and a hundred other small farms like us across the state." The last sentence broke with a sob and she sat on the ottoman, burying her head in her hands. "It's that you didn't choose me," then, she glanced up at him and finished, "again."

26

Harrison closed his eyes to the hurt and the tears on Poppy's face. Is that what he had done? Was he choosing something else over her? Didn't she want him to win? What about all those talks they had about the good they could do with the influence of leadership? Harrison was only trying to do the right thing for the big picture.

"Poppy, I still love you. And I wouldn't want anyone else by my side on this journey. But if this journey isn't going to end with a campaign loss, then I needed to make an ally of Senator Hawkins."

"And you have to break your promise to me to do it?"

Harrison rubbed his jaw, considering. "I don't

know, Poppy. It sure doesn't feel like I have another option."

"Well, you do. And it is to keep your word to your wife. And if lying and trading votes is what it takes to get you to the governor's office, then maybe it isn't where God wants you to be."

Harrison flinched at her words. Of course, God wanted him in the governorship. He wouldn't be doing this if he didn't believe that. But was Poppy right? Was he doing the wrong thing so that he could do the right thing later? He had to believe that God was orchestrating this. Without that, everything up to this point was completely crazy. An arranged marriage and a longshot run for office by the youngest candidate for governor in Indiana history. None of it was logical.

He would still do everything in his power to support small farms. This one bill wasn't going to change that. There would be a hundred bills. He could introduce a separate bill that did even more to help small farms!

"Poppy, I'm just trying to do the best thing here."

She stood, looked him in the eyes, their deep brown depths flashing with gold as she studied him. What was she looking for? Then, her jaw tightened and she nodded once before stepping past him.

Harrison watched her disappear down the dark hallway, the sound of the floor-length dress swishing on the marble floor.

Poppy sat on the edge of the bed, staring at her polished toes peeking out from the glittery dress she'd worn to the fundraiser. Tonight had gone from great to gutter in record time. She thought something was off with Harrison while they got ready before the dinner. He was a completely different person than he had been when he left Monday morning. How had he so easily professed his love for her days before considering turning his back on everything she cared about?

Maybe Stacy was right. Maybe Harrison would always choose his career over a woman. Over her. Still, the connection they had before was real. Her husband did love her. She had to believe that. Even if his actions didn't agree with it. She wanted to leave and go back to the farm.

But what would that get her except a slew of I-told-you-so's from her siblings? Okay, maybe that wasn't fair. Maybe from a few of them, but Poppy knew Lavender would set aside her own feelings to help. Slowly, she changed out of the fancy evening dress and into her leggings. Harrison was nowhere to be seen when she walked back toward the door, so she grabbed her keys and left.

Poppy turned off the music, silencing the mellow indie folk she preferred and sitting in the quiet, with only the purr of the engine. She missed her loud truck. Something caught her eye, the red glow of the dash lights reflected off her wedding ring and she angrily pulled it off her finger and dropped it in the cupholder.

Bloom's farm was quiet, the moon was bright and floodlights illuminated the sides of Storybook Barn as she passed, ambling slowly down the gravel drive all the way to the main house where Rose and Lavender lived with their parents; Hawthorne too, since the bed-and-breakfast was officially open for business.

Poppy texted Lavender so she could let her in the back door. Luckily, Poppy knew her sister stayed up late on the computer most nights, and before long, Lavender opened the door with a confused look on her face.

"What are you doing here?" Lavender asked in a harsh whisper.

"Can we talk?"

They tiptoed back to Lavender's room and shut

the door. "Just a second," she said while she typed something on her computer and then the screen went dark. "Okay. What is this all about, Poppy?"

Poppy sat down, legs crossed and leaning against the wall. "Harrison and I had a fight."

Lavender's face was sympathetic, which only made Poppy feel worse. How could she tell her sister about the fight and not tell her the truth about the marriage? "What about?" Lavender asked.

"What if I told you that Harrison and I didn't get married because of love?"

Lavender's eyes widened and then she shook her head. "That's crazy. You guys are perfect for each other."

Poppy shook her head. "He asked me to marry him so that he would be more electable as governor."

Lavender covered her gasp, "Are you kidding me?" Poppy shook her head in response and Lavender blinked rapidly. "I just... I need a second. He asked you to marry him so he could be governor. But you guys were already dating, so it was just faster than you thought?"

Poppy shook her head again. "It was completely out of the blue, and I don't even know why I said yes, except that it was Harrison and I used to love him so much, and I thought maybe we could have a real future." She blurted out the words, realizing their truth. "I mean, he also promised to vote against the Farm Business Act."

Lavender raised her eyebrows and Poppy hung her head. "I'm an idiot."

Her sister laughed and threw her arm around her. "No, you're not. I mean, this was probably not your best moment, but no one talks about my sister that way."

"He wanted a trophy wife! And I thought I could, I don't know, convince him to love me over time, like some sort of Stockholm syndrome."

"So, he doesn't love you and that's the problem?"

"No, actually, he does love me. Just not enough to choose me over his career." Poppy explained the choice that Harrison had made to vote for the farm bill to save his own legislation.

Her sister winced. "Oh, man. That is pretty awful."

"Right?"

"So now what?" Lavender asked. "I mean, you're already married, right? Are you thinking of walking away?"

"I don't know! Part of me is. Harrison talked such a good game about making a difference together and using his position to show the world Christian leadership. It's so much more influence than I could ever hope to have on my own, you know?"

Lavender scoffed, "You don't need Harrison to make a difference, Poppy."

"Sure I do. Without him, I'm just Poppy Bloom, poor farmer."

"You are so much more than that. You are sister, mentor, daughter, and steward of the land God created! You matter, with or without Harrison. If you do everything you can to make the world a better place and to show the people around you—whether it is two people, or two million—who Jesus is? You have influence."

Poppy considered her sister's words. So often, it felt like what she did hardly made a wrinkle in the grand scheme of things. If Bloom's Farm went away, or wasn't able to grow organic produce anymore, would things really change for people? They would have to get their vegetables from the grocery store, big deal. Memories of the friendly faces she saw each week at the market. Mrs. Dudley and her cute handmade crochet market bags. Mark Dawson and his girlfriend Danielle, who wandered through each week hand-in-hand.

Then there were the orchard events: pick your own apples and berries, pumpkin patches and hayrides. Bloom's Farm was more than produce and Poppy was more than Bloom's Farm. With or without Harrison, she would continue fighting for small farms and showing people who Jesus was. Lavender was right. Poppy had gotten so caught up in the idea that being married to Harrison would give her a voice. But she already had a voice. And she was going to use it.

She and Lavender came up with a plan, and Lavender quickly fired up her computer to help get the word out. It was going to be an interesting week in Indianapolis.

"Thanks, Lavender."

"You know I'm always here for you. So, what are you going to do about the marriage?"

Poppy smiled, "We will see. Harrison is about to see who he is married to. Then we will go from there. I hope he still loves me. But if not, I'll be okay." She spent the night with her sister, then went back home in the morning. Home—the house in Terre Haute she shared with her husband.

27

Harrison stayed in Indianapolis until Saturday, a few days without seeing Poppy after the fundraiser. He couldn't bring himself to come home any sooner, so he called Janet and had her upload any files he needed to work from Indianapolis. Harrison didn't know what to expect when he came home. Would she still be at their little house in Terre Haute? Or would he find empty closets and a disturbing lack of citrus shampoo?

When he came in late on Saturday night, her truck was parked on the street and a light was left on in the hallway. Sunday morning, Poppy got ready for church and walked out to the kitchen, where Harrison drank his coffee and watched a cable news show. He eyed her with surprise when she walked in, her floral print skirt and teal shirt making her the very picture of spring.

"Will you be coming to church with me this morning?" she asked as she poured herself a mug.

Harrison grunted and stood. Better get moving if he was going to attend. He had expected to skip church this morning, or at least for Poppy to want to continue their argument. She was suspiciously good-natured this morning. Maybe she'd forgiven him?

Either way, he knew going to church would be good for him and he hurried to grab a shower and get ready. Wordlessly, they climbed into his car and made the short drive to the large community church she had attended since returning from college. Her parents still went to the small church in Minden. Harrison had been attending another large church in Terre Haute, but didn't mind switching.

Hesitantly, he extended his hand to Poppy as they walked in, relief filling him as she tucked her hand in his. Maybe everything was going to be okay. They filed into the row occupied by her siblings as the song started. Harrison tried to focus on the worship songs, but his mind kept wandering to the short, sweet-natured woman next to him. He didn't deserve her. Or her forgiveness, actually.

He hadn't even asked for it. Yet it seemed like she'd forgiven him.

Harrison had to go back to Indianapolis again tonight. He'd be so glad when this legislative session was over. It seemed to be taking ages. This week was critical though, the vote for the farm bill, and hopefully—his education bill coming out of committee with rousing support.

He glanced at Poppy's profile as she watched the pastor speak. He studied the curve of her chin and lips, her little nose. At his gaze, she turned and gave him a questioning look. He smiled slightly and laid a hand on her thigh. How could he consider turning his back on Poppy and breaking his word? What kind of husband would do that? What kind of leadership did that show?

This was driving him crazy. He'd always tried to do what God intended for him to do. Did God want him to be governor? If so, shouldn't he do the things he needed to in order to make it happen? He wouldn't even be married to Poppy if he wasn't trying to become governor, after all. This week, he would have to decide whether or not to keep his word to Poppy, or basically let his beloved education initiative crash and burn.

Instead of listening to the pastor, Harrison

prayed for guidance. What should he do? Poppy was being pleasant and loving, her hand still rested on his, but just because he was pretty sure she would forgive him, it wouldn't be right to take advantage of her grace. What was it that Paul said? Shall we use grace as an excuse to sin? Harrison desperately needed wisdom. What was he supposed to do when he felt like God was pulling him in two directions?

28

Four days later, he'd heard nothing from Poppy since he left for the city on Sunday night. Harrison walked up the steps to the Indiana statehouse in the cool morning air, unsurprised to see a group of protesters in front of the statehouse. There were often groups there supporting various causes with homemade signs and flyers they tried to pass out. This group seemed well organized though, and larger than some. What were they protesting? The only thing on the docket this morning was the farm bill.

Then, a flash of a familiar auburn braid caught his eye. Was that? Yep. Harrison immediately resurveyed the ragtag group of protesters. A man and three young children close to him caught his eye, "Andrew?"

"Senator!" Andrew Treat exclaimed. "Good to see you! When Poppy called me, I was surprised to hear you were on board with this kind of demonstration, but I think it's amazing. My wife would love to be here, but the baby is not being very considerate, you know?"

Honestly, Harrison had no idea, but he nodded his head. Poppy's voice rang across the space, and she led the group in a chant, "Small farms feed Indiana!"

Harrison watched her, his smile broadening at her rosy cheeks in the chilly April air. Her eyes were bright and smiling like he hadn't seen since the Harvest Festival in Minden. The wind blew a few wisps of hair into her face, and she brushed them aside. She was beautiful. Her gaze locked on Harrison's, and she froze as the rest of the protesters continued to march around her. Poppy smiled and shrugged. Harrison felt a tug on his pant leg, an adorable toddler with blonde hair and the biggest blue eyes he had ever seen.

"Do you like my sign?" she asked, holding a small sign on a stick. It had two small handprints, presumably her own and said "Small hands. Small farms. Big difference."

Harrison kneeled down, "I love your sign! Did you help make it?"

With that, the little girl was off on a long story about making her sign until Andrew laid a hand on her head. "Okay, little one. Let Mister Harrison talk to Miss Poppy for a moment."

Harrison stood to find Poppy next to him.

"Good morning, Senator," she said. His lips twitched at the formality.

"Mind telling me what this is all about, Mrs. Coulter?" Two could play that game.

"Someone reminded me that I don't have to be married to a governor or a senator to make a difference. So, we are making our voices heard this morning before you vote on the Farm Business Act."

Poppy was adorable when she was feisty. He raised his eyebrow in mock condescension, "Is this supposed to change my mind?" Harrison was already pretty sure he knew what he was going to do, but he wanted to know what Poppy thought would happen.

Poppy shrugged and looked around. "No more than it should every other senator who walks by us this morning. These are the faces of the farmers who the farm bill would put in jeopardy. I hope you and your colleagues will consider that while voting."

Harrison smiled at her passionate argument and

stepped close. "You know I love you, right?" he asked quietly. Poppy's smiled bloomed, and she ducked her head in a nod. "Good. And I love that you are here fighting for what you believe in."

The surprise was written on Poppy's face. "You do? I kind of thought you might be upset. After all, there is a reporter on her way, and I am your wife..." Her words died as Harrison covered her mouth with his. He was surprised a reporter would be covering the protest, but it didn't matter. Poppy was her own person, capable of standing up for her own beliefs. And Harrison was proud to have a woman like that by his side, even if they would disagree on things from time to time.

Poppy leaned into the kiss, and Harrison dropped his briefcase to hold her close as Andrew and his children hooted encouragement. Whatever happened inside that stateroom today, Harrison had everything he needed right here in his arms. Maybe God was calling him to run for governor. Or maybe God was just delivering an unconventional wake-up call in the form of marriage to an unconventional woman.

When they finally broke the kiss, he tucked Poppy under his chin and kissed the top of her head. "Have dinner with me tonight," he said. It was probably rude to not ask, but he didn't want to leave her room to say no. After everything that was about to happen, whether he propelled his career forward and dimmed the light in Poppy's eyes, or if he watched his political hopes be dashed, there was no one he would rather see in the aftermath.

"I really should get back to the farm after this," Poppy shook her head.

"Have dinner with me tonight," Harrison said again. Then, with a teasing grin, he added, "Please?"

Poppy smiled, "Okay. I'll be at the mausoleum," she joked.

"Can't wait."

"Tell me, Mrs. Coulter, why are you here today?" The reporter held a microphone with a big red top on it and Poppy tried to swallow the nerves that threatened.

"I'm here to support small farms across the state of Indiana. As the senate votes this morning on SB 245—The Farm Business Act, they hold the future of Indiana's family-owned farms in their hands."

"One of those very senators is your husband,

Harrison Coulter, is it not? Can you tell us how he is voting?"

Poppy shook her head, "I know how I would like him to vote, but I also know that regardless of the outcome of this particular bill, my husband, Senator Coulter, will do his very best to act in the interest of farmers and the state of Indiana as a whole." There, that sounded good, right? Would it give Harrison enough wiggle room if he ended up voting against the bill? Still, she was desperately hoping he would stand with her. She would try her best to understand and forgive him if he didn't, but it would sting. Oh, man. It would definitely sting.

Poppy twisted her ring around her finger and answered a few more questions for the reporter about Bloom's Farm and the importance of local farming. Those were easy, and she spoke straight from her heart.

Would Harrison see this interview? Would he approve of her actions? It had been a huge relief to see him this morning and hear his reassurance that he loved her. When she spotted him across the small crowd, her heart had frozen in her chest. She feared his disapproval. But his simple affirmation had been exactly what she needed. It was confirmation that their relationship could survive this, no matter what the outcome. Maybe that was what God was trying to show them. Surely, if Harrison were governor, he would have to do things that Poppy didn't agree with. She couldn't hold a grudge every single time. That was no way to build a strong marriage.

Her agreement with Harrison may have started out as transactional, but now? It was so much more than that. As long as she reminded herself that Harrison was the man that she loved and would choose to love every day moving forward? It would be okay.

29

Harrison left his chat with Poppy still feeling torn. On one hand, he had everything he had been working for—all he had to do was vote for the farm bill and he would have bipartisan support for his education bill. A success like that could carry him to the governor's office.

On the other hand, he had Poppy and the promise that he had made to her. He had the ideals he had stood for from the beginning and the face of Andrew Treat's precious daughter and her homemade sign. Could he, in good conscience, vote for a bill that would hurt small farms?

Harrison's first stop when he got inside was his office. His assistant handed him a small stack of call slips and then, an envelope with his name scrawled across it in blue ink. "Someone left this for you," was all his assistant said before returning to her desk and leaving him at his.

Curiosity got the better of him and he ignored the stack of papers, a quick glance showing several were from Senator Hawkins's office. He pulled the letter out, leaned back in the cushioned leather chair, and started to read.

When he reached the end of the letter, Harrison called Bethany. "Keep me posted on the expected votes if you hear anything."

"How are you going to vote, Senator?"

"I guess we will all find out when the time comes," he replied.

Thirty minutes later, as Harrison pretended to read a document from the blue chair of his official Senate chamber desk, every text message from Bethany made it clear that Harrison was likely to be the tie-breaking vote.

The gavel sounded, and Harrison leaned back in the blue leather chair. He listened to the Lieutenant Governor introduce the bill and open the floor. Senator Hawkins stood up, and Harrison tuned out as he droned on in his monotone voice. Harrison sent a prayer toward the ceiling of the chamber, hoping he was doing the right thing. His entire journey into politics had been because God gave him the call. Had he strayed from that? Did God want him to be the governor? Or was it only his own ambition that had him climbing the political ladder?

Senators around him applauded something Hawkins said, and Harrison tried again to at least appear like he was paying attention. Hawkins seemed to zero in on him as he spoke, their eyes meeting across the chamber. "I trust all of my esteemed colleagues from around the state will see how *beneficial* this bill will be to the *future*." His emphasis was not lost on Harrison, a loosely veiled threat at best. Hawkins would do everything in his power to tank the education bill if Harrison voted against.

Which was ridiculous. The TEACH Act was a good piece of legislation. Harrison and his team had worked for countless hours, reading reports on what teachers needed and the best practices of other states. It should pass with overwhelming support. But Harrison knew that *should* didn't always mean a lot when it came to politics. Senators *should* vote for the best thing, even if it was across party lines.

Hawkins finally stopped talking and someone called for a vote to end discussion. Harrison pushed the small green button at the front of his desk; this was an easy one. This vote would only end any debates, and then the real vote on the issue would happen.

He chatted with Senator Franklin, who shared his table, and waited for the tally. Thankfully, the debate was over and the real voting would begin. The Lieutenant Governor announced the five-minute voting time and wracked his gavel.

Harrison stared at the green button. Governorship. The difference he could make. A broken promise. His gaze slid right to the red button. Poppy. Andrew Treat. Keeping his word. A battle against Hawkins for the TEACH Act.

Time was ticking down. Harrison looked up from his desk to see Hawkins moseying over. He stood next to Harrison's desk.

"I don't see a light next to your name, Senator Coulter," he hissed quietly.

"Nope, I'm still thinking." Not about how to vote, but that was beside the point. Harrison had known exactly how he would vote from the moment he read the letter in his office.

Hawkins's jaw clinched and he leaned over, wagging his finger far too close to Harrison's face. Harrison could see the perspiration on Hawkins's forehead and recognized the anxiety in his face. "You better listen to me, Coulter. I own this town, and I will personally make sure you are nothing more than a two-bit has-been senator if you cross me. So help me God—"

Harrison stood, coming to his full height, several inches taller than Senator Hawkins. "Maybe God will help, you, Hawkins. He's certainly helped me know exactly how I should vote on this issue."

And with that, Harrison leaned over and pushed the red button as Hawkins's mouth fell open and his eyes bulged. He stammered and stuttered before finally pounding a fist on Harrison's table. "We are *not* done."

Harrison watched him walk away and shook his head. Hawkins seemed to have an awful lot riding on this bill. Either way, Harrison was done being a pawn in his game. If God wanted him to be governor, he would just have to do it in spite of Hawkins. Why he had thought Hawkins would be such a huge obstacle, he didn't know. Of course God could still install Harrison as governor. Nothing would stand against God's plans. Not even a manipulative senator who thought he could control everything.

The Lieutenant governor rapped his gavel and announced the results of the voting. "With a vote of 49 for, 50 against, and 1 abstention, SB 245 fails to advance. With that, we will recess for lunch. Session will reconvene at 14:00."

A broad smile spread across Harrison's face. On the solid oak desk in front of him, Harrison's phone vibrated and lit up. Poppy's name caught his eye and he tapped on the message notification.

Thank you.

Harrison tapped back a quick reply.

It was the right thing to do. I'm sorry it took me so long to recognize it.

I'm so proud of you.

Whatever the outcome, Harrison knew he could rest in the respect and approval of his wife. And he could sleep at night, at peace with his own decision. **This might cost us the governorship.**

Only a moment passed before her reply, **I love you. And you've got my vote.**

Harrison slid his phone into his pocket and made his way out of the senate chambers, shaking hands with other senators who voted against the bill, and stepping into the marble rotunda where he immediately spotted Poppy waiting for him. She stood in the very center of the circle demarcating the rotunda, the very spot where he'd kissed her in the soft glow of the chandeliers.

She smiled sweetly at him, her cheeks still pink from the cold outside. "Hello again, Senator."

Harrison wrapped his arms around her and she tipped her head up towards him. "Care to have lunch, beautiful?"

Poppy blushed, and he kissed her warmly, ignoring the desire to deepen the kiss, well aware of the reporters and curious glances they had already received.

"I'd love to."

~

Harrison,

When you asked me to marry you, I thought you'd lost your mind. Now, I know I've lost my heart.

I married a man doing his best to follow God's leading. A man full of honor and conviction. Sometimes stubborn, and sometimes so incredibly tender it turns me inside out.

Senator Coulter, vote today however you need to. I hereby release you from any agreement we may have had regarding this vote. I do not, however, release you from the other agreement we made: our promises to love and honor, cherish, protect, and encourage each other.

No matter what happens today, I am proud of you. No matter what happens tomorrow, I'll choose you. No matter what happens in fifty years, I'll be there for you. I love you.

I'll see you soon, my dear husband. My prayers are with you!

-Poppy

30

Two weeks later, Poppy held her gloves in one hand as she watched the livestream of the senate session, something she never thought she would do, as Harrison's education bill came up for a vote. Despite an attempt to squash the bill during committee, Senator Hawkins hadn't been able to do it. Turns out, more than one senator was tired of being pushed around by the despicable man. Still, even though Harrison had done everything he could, including private meetings and dinners with almost every senator in the state and rallying support from every Parent Teacher Association and teachers' union he could, it could come down to the wire on whether the bill passed.

From her sturdy wooden bench in the large greenhouse where she was transplanting tomato seedlings, she watched the numbers tally at the bottom of her tiny screen. Come on, come on. The timer counted down, only two minutes of voting left. But the Ayes were ticking up steadily, almost there.

When Poppy saw the total cross fifty-one, she tossed her gardening gloves in the air with a loud shout of celebration. He had done it! Pride swelled within her as the senate chambers erupted in applause, and she could see Harrison from the overview camera, shaking hands and taking well-deserved slaps on the shoulder as senators came to offer their congratulations. The positive votes continued rolling in, and Harrison's bill had passed by a landslide. She quickly exited the browser and sent him a text.

Congratulations! I love you!

She didn't expect an answer soon and went back to her seedlings. The tiny tomato plants were roughly six inches high, and nearly ready to be planted outside in the rich soil of the vegetable field. The early starters were nearly a foot high and would bear some early season fruit within the month for her to include in the CSA baskets.

Within the hour, Poppy's phone rang. Eagerly,

she grabbed the phone with gloved hands and accepted the call with her nose before continuing to weed the cucumbers.

Harrison's voice was breathy and excited. "Poppy, are you there?"

"I'm here. I'm so happy for you!"

"Thank you, I am still riding the wave, I think. It still seems a bit surreal." It felt like she had barely seen him in the last two weeks. She'd even stayed at the condo in the city a few nights, just so they could spend some time together, but between him trying to personally convince every senator why they should vote for his bill and her trying to manage the early planting season, it was very limited. "When can you get here?" he asked.

Poppy straightened and grabbed the phone, ignoring the dirt that fell to her shoulder from her glove. "What?"

"Neil suggested I host the press conference today and announce my run for governor. It's a few months ahead of schedule, but we've got momentum. What do you think? Can you make it?"

Poppy glanced around the greenhouse, the wind snapping against the plastic sheeting. Clyde and Lewis were out planting sweet corn and watermelons, and there was still a ton of work to be done here.

Could she go to the capital today? “I don't know, I'm pretty busy here. You can make the announcement without me, though,” she offered.

“No, no. That's okay. We don't have to announce it today. But Poppy?”

“Yeah?”

“There is no way I'm announcing this without you by my side.”

“Because of the optics?” she asked nervously.

“Screw the optics,” he said harshly and Poppy covered a laugh, “I love you and there is no one I would rather have next to me when I announce. We will do it whenever it works.”

Poppy's smile broadened and she pulled off her gloves, glancing down at her dirt-stained khaki shorts. A shower and a change of clothes was in order. “I'll be there in three hours.”

She heard Harrison chuckle, “Are you sure?”

Poppy headed toward the door. “Two hours and fifty-nine minutes, Coulter. Count 'em.”

“Okay, then. I'll see you soon.”

“See you. Oh, and Harrison? I love you, too.”

~

Harrison stood behind the small podium temporarily set up on the steps of the statehouse and smiled at the small cluster of reporters and cameramen who had gathered. Behind him, Poppy stood tall with her hands clasped in front of her. Neil, Bethany, and a small team of his staff and supporters filled the background.

"Thank you for coming, everyone. It's been a very exciting day here at the capital. The final day of the senate session and the passing of landmark legislation that will make recruiting and rewarding our teachers easier than ever. I would like to thank all of my colleagues from the house and the senate for agreeing on the importance of the TEACH Act. Our schools and students will be better prepared to succeed thanks to your support.

"I would also like to take this moment to announce my candidacy for governor of Indiana. When I entered public service as a city councilman eight years ago, I never thought I would become a state senator. I was convinced that my place to make a difference was in the courtroom, fighting for justice there. But over the past six years, God has continued to call me into bigger steps of faith and increasingly large roles within government service. I believe it is crucially important at this moment in history for our state to remain grounded in the ideals we stand on, and that we value integrity and character above all else. Without integrity, nothing else matters.

"I look forward to setting out on the campaign trail and meeting even more of the strong, hard-working Hoosiers who make this state great. I am honored to do so with my amazing wife, Poppy, who always stands by me and reminds me of the most important things. Being your governor would be an immense honor and an immense responsibility, one I would not take lightly. I promise to do the right thing for this state, even when it is difficult, or unpopular. In the face of opposition, I stood my ground and stood up for small farms and businesses. Garnering bi-partisan support, I spearheaded groundbreaking legislation that will ensure our education system is strong and supported for years ahead.

"I look forward to doing even more as the next governor of the great state of Indiana."

A smattering of applause rose and Harrison stepped back from the microphone, gesturing for Poppy to step toward him. He knew that at his last words, Neil had pulled a small string and unrolled the large 'Coulter for Governor' banner behind him. It was official, Harrison was running for governor.

He slipped his arm around Poppy and posed for a couple of pictures for the reporters.

Poppy looked up at him and he studied her face. "What do you say we go home?"

"Home sounds perfect," she responded.

At his apartment, Poppy kicked off the cotton canvas flats she'd worn and collapsed onto the low-slung leather couch. Harrison loosened his tie and motioned for her to lean up so he could sit next to her. Then he pulled her back down so she rested comfortably on his shoulder. He ran his fingers through her hair, and she closed her eyes. He traced a finger down her sun-kissed cheek, trailing over her lips with a knuckle.

She smiled at the contact and opened her eyes, her brown eyes melting him with their power. Gently, he tucked his finger under her chin and tipped her head up to him, then leaned down and pressed his lips against hers.

"I love you," he whispered.

"I love you."

"Will you marry me?" he asked.

Poppy smiled. "We're already married, Senator."

"I know. But I want to marry you again, in a church in front of our family. Whatever."

She sat up and turned toward him. "I don't want

to redo our vows. I meant every word I said. I might not have known exactly what it would look like, but I said them with my eyes wide open. Our journey might be a bit unconventional, but God brought us together, and I wouldn't have done it any other way."

"Are you sure?" he asked. "Don't you want a big party? Do it for real?"

"It was real then. There is one thing that I do want, Harrison." Poppy looked up at him, her dark brown eyes pulling him in.

"Anything," he said without hesitation.

"I want to be your wife. Fully." A blush rose in her cheeks and Harrison felt his mouth go dry. Was Poppy saying what he thought she was saying?

"Poppy, we don't have to—"

His words were cut off as Poppy rose to her knees on the couch and pressed her lips against his. He brushed his hands along her waist, the soft cotton fabric caressing his fingers. He flattened his palm against the small of her back and she melted into him, taking the kiss deeper. There was nothing except this moment, the entire world could come crashing down outside of his apartment window and Harrison would not have noticed, or cared. There were only her lips on his own, her body pressed against his, and the marvel of knowing Poppy was his, truly his, forever.

For some reason, God had given him the remarkable gift of the woman in his arms. A wife who loved him, respected him, and desired him. Whatever the outcome of the election, Harrison knew he had already been given everything.

EPILOGUE

Nearly six months had passed since Keith's stroke. Laura Bloom made herself a cup of coffee and watched the sun rise over the hills behind her house, golden sunlight just barely streaming over the horizon and shining through her kitchen windows.

Keith was still sleeping, the early riser she'd married now required early nights and later mornings. Their entire lives, he'd worked sunup to sundown, tirelessly caring for animals and crops, baling hay and harvesting corn. And somehow, still redeeming pockets of time for each of their children and investing himself in them.

Poppy and Rose, especially, had been Daddy's little girls, each grasping on to their own little segment of the farm and spending time with Keith to learn it inside and out. After Poppy came home from college with a degree in agronomy horticulture, she'd helped them make the transition to certified organic.

Now, Laura didn't know what would happen. Poppy had gotten married. And Laura already loved Harrison; he was hard not to like. He definitely had charisma. Last week, he'd announced his candidacy for governor. Poppy and Harrison had mentioned it was likely, but it was still something that caught you off guard.

Her daughter, her precious Poppy—so often content to be one of the crowd—could be the next first lady of the state. When she'd seen Poppy on the news that night, it had been almost surreal. But she'd seen the way Harrison looked at her daughter, love and adoration plain in his eyes. Laura didn't know the whole truth about the origins of Poppy's relationship with Harrison. It had been too secretive and fast to have been easily explained away. However they had come together, Poppy and Harrison were poised to take on forever.

What would that mean for the farm? Keith was doing his best to help where he could, the farm air and the normalcy strengthened him each day, but the effects of his stroke lingered. Probably slight enough to be overlooked by most, but glaringly obvious to the woman who'd spent her life waking up next to him each day. Laura knew God would bring the right person to the farm to manage the produce operation. For the first time in generations, though, that person might not be a Bloom. Whoever God brought, Laura would welcome them with open arms. God knew who the farm needed. And who needed the farm.

Now, if only Lavender could peek out from behind her computer and embrace things in the real world. From the little room where Laura worked on the finances for the farm, she could hear Lavender chatting with her online friends, making videos or something. When she was on camera, safely hidden behind a screen, Lavender transformed from a shy, reserved woman to a bold, knowledgeable marketing expert with a fun, quirky sense of humor. But how would anyone ever see the beautiful spirit she carried if she couldn't open up in person?

Poppy was married, Hawthorne was engaged, and Daisy seemed to have found her perfect match. But Lavender seemed perfectly content to spend her hours online. Laura reminded herself to trust God to bring the perfect someone into her daughter's life.

ABOUT LAVENDER AND LACE

Book 3 in The Bloom Sisters Series

In their online writer chatroom, they are getting serious.
In the real world; He thinks she's shallow, and she thinks he's out of touch.
When their worlds collide, will their hearts survive?

Lavender Bloom is a social marketing expert and influential fashion blogger. Always focused on the perfect image, she shows the world a flawless version of herself, except to her family and her nameless online best friend. Her broody new client certainly doesn't understand her or why she prefers to hide behind her computer.

Reclusive author Emmett Drake spends his days writing his award-winning fantasy saga and his nights chatting online with the woman of his dreams. When he is forced to hire an image consultant to please his publisher, he despises everything the woman stands for, even if he sees hidden depths beneath her polished façade.

Lavender is determined to help Emmett embrace the power of social media. Meanwhile, he is determined to uncover the woman hiding behind the carefully scripted marketing lingo. Their struggle to find authenticity in a world centered on likes, comments, and shares will challenge them both to embrace God's purpose for their lives – together.

Return to Bloom's Farm in Lavender and Lace and embrace the joy of family, faith, and true love in this nostalgic modern nod to the romantic classic, You've Got Mail.

ACKNOWLEDGMENTS

Thank you, Precious Savior for the abundant life you've given me. I know I don't deserve it. Fill me with a deeper appreciation of the Gospel so I might grow in faith and fruit.

To my editor, Jessica from BH Writing Services. I treasure our time together, and I'm so proud of the business you've established! Thanks for your insight and encouragement.

Special thanks to Katie W, for talking me through a courthouse wedding and providing a copy of the actual vows you said. That scene would have been far lacking without your help!

Thanks also to my sister-in-law, Tracie, for insight on her own courthouse wedding!

To Susan and Judy for proofreading. Any remaining errors are entirely my own.

To Gabbi, you never cease to make me smile.

To Hannah Jo Abbott Mandi Blake, for being on your own crazy version of this author adventure, and sharing it every day.

And to the rest of our Author circle -- Jess Mastorakos, Elizabeth Maddrey and K Leah -- Thank you for the random chats, the accountability, the cheerleading, and the writing sprints.

To my parents, who didn't flinch when I decided to chase dreams I never expected to have.

To the women of Fellowship Bible Church and our devoted group, thank you for your prayers and your support. Coming into your group two years ago felt like coming home.

Thank you to all my readers, without whose support and encouragement, I would have given up a long time ago.

And finally, to my husband. I'm so grateful for your support, love, and endless grace.

Mr. B and Little C; you are getting so big. I love you to the moon and back.

NOTE TO READERS

Note to Readers

Thank you for picking up (or downloading!) this book. If you enjoyed it, please consider taking a minute to leave a review – it would literally make me do a happy dance!

It was fun for me to write a marriage of convenience story – I love to read them! I especially valued how Poppy and Harrison went into the relationship knowing that love was a choice, and that marriage was forever – even if it started as a contract. And watching God open their eyes to their own blind spots helped me see a few of my own. I pray my books encourage you in your faith and through your struggles, whatever they may be.

You can learn more about my upcoming projects at my website: www.taragraceericson.com or by signing up for my newsletter. Just for signing up, you will get a free story!

If you've never read my other books, I'd love for you to read the Main Street Minden Series and dive into the world of Minden, Indiana. Or, read more about the Bloom Family in Hoping for Hawthorne and A Date for Daisy

Thank you again for all your support and encouragement.

BOOKS BY TARA GRACE ERICSON

The Main Street Minden Series

Falling on Main Street

Winter Wishes

Spring Fever

Summer to Remember

Kissing in the Kitchen: A Main Street Minden Novella

The Bloom Sisters Series

Hoping for Hawthorne - A Bloom Family Novella

A Date for Daisy

Poppy's Proposal

Made in the USA
Middletown, DE
29 August 2021

46829938R00182